FRA

DAR

M000211699

Francis Vivian was born Arthur Ernest Ashley in 1906 at East Retford, Nottinghamshire. He was the younger brother of noted photographer Hallam Ashley. Vivian laboured for a decade as a painter and decorator before becoming an author of popular fiction in 1932. In 1940 he married schoolteacher Dorothy Wallwork, and the couple had a daughter.

After the Second World War he became assistant editor at the Nottinghamshire Free Press and circuit lecturer on many subjects, ranging from crime to bee-keeping (the latter forming a major theme in the Inspector Knollis mystery *The Singing Masons*). A founding member of the Nottingham Writers' Club, Vivian once awarded first prize in a writing competition to a young Alan Sillitoe, the future bestselling author.

The ten Inspector Knollis mysteries were published between 1941 and 1956. In the novels, ingenious plotting and fair play are paramount. A colleague recalled that 'the reader could always arrive at a correct solution from the given data. Inspector Knollis never picked up an undisclosed clue which, it was later revealed, held the solution to the mystery all along.'

Francis Vivian died on April 2, 1979 at the age of 73.

THE INSPECTOR KNOLLIS MYSTERIES
Available from Dean Street Press

FRANCIS VIVIAN

DARKLING DEATH

With an introduction by Curtis Evans

DEAN STREET PRESS

Published by Dean Street Press 2018

First published in 1956 by Herbert Jenkins Ltd.

Cover by DSP

ISBN 978 1 912574 45 2

www.deanstreetpress.co.uk

INTRODUCTION

SHORTLY BEFORE his death in 1951, American agriculturalist and scholar Everett Franklin Phillips, then Professor Emeritus of Apiculture (beekeeping) at Cornell University, wrote British newspaperman Arthur Ernest Ashley (1906-1979), author of detective novels under the pseudonym Francis Vivian, requesting a copy of his beekeeping mystery *The Singing Masons*, the sixth Inspector Gordon Knollis investigation, which had been published the previous year in the United Kingdom. The eminent professor wanted the book for Cornell's Everett F. Phillips Beekeeping Collection, "one of the largest and most complete apiculture libraries in the world" (currently in the process of digitization at Cornell's The Hive and the Honeybee website). Sixteen years later Ernest Ashely, or Francis Vivian as I shall henceforward name him, to an American fan requesting an autograph ("Why anyone in the United States, where I am not known," he self-deprecatingly observed, "should want my autograph I cannot imagine, but I am flattered by your request and return your card, duly signed.") declared that fulfilling Professor Phillip's donation request was his "greatest satisfaction as a writer." With ghoulish relish he added, "I believe there was some objection by the Librarian, but the good doctor insisted, and so in it went! It was probably destroyed after Dr. Phillips died. Stung to death."

After investigation I have found no indication that the August 1951 death of Professor Phillips, who was 73 years old at the time, was due to anything other than natural causes. One assumes that what would have been the painfully ironic demise of the American nation's most distinguished apiculturist from bee stings would have merited some mention in his death notices. Yet Francis Vivian's fabulistic claim otherwise provides us with a glimpse of that mordant sense of humor and storytelling relish which glint throughout the eighteen mystery novels Vivian published between 1937 and 1959.

Ten of these mysteries were tales of the ingenious sleuthing exploits of series detective Inspector Gordon Knollis, head of the Burnham C.I.D. in the first novel in the series and a Scotland Yard detective in the rest. (Knollis returns to Burnham in later novels.) The debut Inspector Knollis mystery, *The Death of Mr. Lomas,* which was published in 1941, is actually the seventh Francis Vivian detective novel. However, after the Second World War, when the author belatedly returned to his vocation of mystery writing, all of the remaining detective novels he published, with two exceptions, chronicle the criminal cases of the keen and clever Knollis. These other Inspector Knollis tales are: *Sable Messenger* (1947), *The Threefold Cord* (1947), *The Ninth Enemy* (1948), *The Laughing Dog* (1949), *The Singing Masons* (1950), *The Elusive Bowman* (1951), *The Sleeping Island* (1951), *The Ladies of Locksley* (1953) and *Darkling Death* (1956). (Inspector Knollis also is passingly mentioned in Francis Vivian's final mystery, published in 1959, *Dead Opposite the Church.*) By the late Forties and early Fifties, when Hodder & Stoughton, one of England's most important purveyors of crime and mystery fiction, was publishing the Francis Vivian novels, the Inspector Knollis mysteries had achieved wide popularity in the UK, where "according to the booksellers and librarians," the author's newspaper colleague John Hall later recalled in the *Guardian* (possibly with some exaggeration), "Francis Vivian was neck and neck with Ngaio Marsh in second place after Agatha Christie." (Hardcover sales and penny library rentals must be meant here, as with one exception--a paperback original--Francis Vivian, in great contrast with Crime Queens Marsh and Christie, both mainstays of Penguin Books in the UK, was never published in softcover.)

John Hall asserted that in Francis Vivian's native coal and iron county of Nottinghamshire, where Vivian from the 1940s through the 1960s was an assistant editor and "colour man" (writer of local color stories) on the Nottingham, or Notts, *Free Press,* the detective novelist "through a large stretch of the coalfield is reckoned the best local author after Byron and D. H. Lawrence." Hall added that "People who wouldn't know Alan

Sillitoe from George Eliot will stop Ernest in the street and tell him they solved his last detective story." Somewhat ironically, given this assertion, Vivian in his capacity as a founding member of the Nottingham Writers Club awarded first prize in a 1950 Nottingham writing competition to no other than 22-year-old local aspirant Alan Sillitoe, future "angry young man" author of *Saturday Night and Sunday Morning* (1958) and *The Loneliness of the Long Distance Runner* (1959). In his 1995 autobiography Sillitoe recollected that Vivian, "a crime novelist who earned his living by writing . . . gave [my story] first prize, telling me it was so well written and original that nothing further need be done, and that I should try to get it published." This was "The General's Dilemma," which Sillitoe later expanded into his second novel, *The General* (1960).

While never himself an angry young man (he was, rather, a "ragged-trousered" philosopher), Francis Vivian came from fairly humble origins in life and well knew how to wield both the hammer and the pen. Born on March 23, 1906, Vivian was one of two children of Arthur Ernest Ashley, Sr., a photographer and picture framer in East Retford, Nottinghamshire, and Elizabeth Hallam. His elder brother, Hallam Ashley (1900-1987), moved to Norwich and became a freelance photographer. Today he is known for his photographs, taken from the 1940s through the 1960s, chronicling rural labor in East Anglia (many of which were collected in the 2010 book *Traditional Crafts and Industries in East Anglia: The Photographs of Hallam Ashley*). For his part, Francis Vivian started working at age 15 as a gas meter emptier, then labored for 11 years as a housepainter and decorator before successfully establishing himself in 1932 as a writer of short fiction for newspapers and general magazines. In 1937, he published his first detective novel, *Death at the Salutation*. Three years later, he wed schoolteacher Dorothy Wallwork, with whom he had one daughter.

After the Second World War Francis Vivian's work with the Notts *Free Press* consumed much of his time, yet he was still able for the next half-dozen years to publish annually a detective novel (or two), as well as to give popular lectures on a plethora of intriguing subjects, including, naturally enough, crime, but also fiction writing (he published two guidebooks on that subject), psychic forces (he believed himself to be psychic), black magic, Greek civilization, drama, psychology and beekeeping. The latter occupation he himself took up as a hobby, following in the path of Sherlock Holmes. Vivian's fascination with such esoterica invariably found its way into his detective novels, much to the delight of his loyal readership.

As a detective novelist, John Hall recalled, Francis Vivian "took great pride in the fact that the reader could always arrive at a correct solution from the given data. His Inspector never picked up an undisclosed clue which, it was later revealed, held the solution to the mystery all along." Vivian died on April 2, 1979, at the respectable if not quite venerable age of 73, just like Professor Everett Franklin Phillips. To my knowledge the late mystery writer had not been stung to death by bees.

Curtis Evans

I
Enigmatic Journey

BROTHER IGNATIUS was always too early for appointments, meals, and trains, so that he was sitting in the east-bound train at Liverpool Street a full twenty minutes before it was due to leave for East Anglia, and the engine-driver, or perhaps it was the fireman, was amusing himself, or so it seemed to the little priest, by letting off steam every few minutes, to the apparent amusement of a youngish man, probably no more than thirty, who stood on the platform with a rucksack at his feet, a much-travelled Burberry over his left shoulder, and a pipe and box of matches which he was trying to bring together into effective use against the strong draught that was whipping down the length of the platform.

So that he should not be tempted to make private guesses about the man's profession and business, for such vulgarity was forbidden to him by the rules of his order, the little priest opened his valise, took out a well-used and heavy volume, and plunged into what was perhaps his thirteenth excursion into Lahsen's theory of recurring lives, a modification of the eternal recurrence philosophy previously taught by Peter Damian Ouspensky. His eyes refused to remain focused on the print, for his mind was not fully with Lahsen this morning. His thoughts tended to scatter instead of canalise, and he was uncomfortably aware of an inner restlessness and unease that on previous occasions had preceded events far different from those that generally made up the come-day go-day routine of his existence.

He knew something was going to happen, something intimately connected with the humorous-eyed and lightly-moustached man on the platform, and that he himself would be inextricably bound up in it.

Why this was so, he could not have explained. Perhaps both Lahsen and Ouspensky were correct, and we did, each of us, continue to live the same life over and over again.

It was a heinous theory, the invention of a mind more horrible than that of Torquemada, and yet had the saving grace of presenting a way out, the possibility of intervention by a neutral observer which could change the course of the repetitive concatenation of lives upon the upward-swirling spiral of eternity.

Brother Ignatius stirred in sympathy with the rising tide of activity on the platform. Porters with trollies were moving into life, although seemingly reluctantly. Passengers were crowding up and down the platform, peering through windows, and passing on to peer through others, as if looking for a compartment in which some previous and unlucky passenger had left a full luncheon basket, or a five-pound note.

The tweed-clad man grasped his rucksack and swung it and himself into the compartment. The rucksack went up to the rack with a practised swing, and the Burberry followed it. The man himself sank down into the corner opposite Brother Ignatius, and gave a friendly smile. "If no one else gets in we're all right."

"No one else will get in," said Brother Ignatius, and immediately wondered why he had said that. Judging by the state of the platform there was every possibility that the compartment would be filled before the guard signalled off the train.

But the doors were slammed with professional vigour, a whistle was blown, and the early morning train to the eastern counties drew out of the station.

"So we really have it to ourselves!"

Brother Ignatius nodded. "You still have me, and you so obviously wanted solitude."

"You don't disturb me—thanks. You aren't that kind of man."

"I trust not. My name, by the way, is Ignatius—Brother Ignatius. I am a priest, a Nestorian priest."

"I'm known as Failure," said the tweedy man. He struck a match and made a further abortive attempt to light the tobacco. "You don't mind if I smoke, Brother?" he asked, with a second match poised over the bowl of his pipe.

"On the contrary. I smoke myself. I think I will indulge myself."

He fidgeted a tin cigarette box from the pocket of his cassock, chose a cigarette with great care, and accepted Failure's offer of a light. He sat back with the cigarette held between his thumb and finger as if it was a stick of chalk with which he was about to draw on a blackboard.

"You are known as Failure," he said flatly.

"My baptismal name is Brandreth Grayson. Failure is only my abysmal name among my friends and relatives."

Brother Ignatius eased the elastic-sided black boots from his feet, and slid forward to rest the heels of his chequered socks on the edge of the opposite seat. They only just reached.

"You are going to Wingford Manor?" he said.

Grayson raised one eyebrow, and ran a hand through his short-cut curly brown hair. "Now how the devil did you guess that—if you'll pardon my mention of the name of your traditional enemy."

Brother Ignatius chuckled. "But for your Satanic friend I should be unemployed—and whoever heard of a priest on the dole? For the rest, I somewhat infrequently visit a member of my flock who lives in Wingford village. A goodly old soul, but I fear a born gossip. Old Mrs. Walters. She lives not far from the Barley Mow, and behind the church. The Barley Mow is where you have stayed on Saturday nights for the past three weeks, is it not?"

Grayson stretched long legs across the compartment and put feet, socks, boots and all on the middle of the seat, sending up a small puff of grey dust.

"Then you know the rest of the story, Brother?"

"From Mrs. Walters, and the London papers. I probably know more than you would prefer the rest of the world to know."

Grayson puffed steadily at his pipe for a time.

"I see you have Lahsen there. I'd recognise him a mile away. You must have had a fair experience of all sides of life, so what do you think of him?"

Brother Ignatius blew a mouthful of smoke down his nose. "Lahsen says much about many things, as did Ouspensky and Georgi Gurdjieff before him, if it comes to that. I suggest that the recent events in your life have bent your thoughts towards one especial aspect of Lahsen's philosophy. You mean, of course, what do I think of his theory of recurring lives?"

"Just that," Grayson replied shortly.

"Truthfully, I find myself in a dilemma," said Brother Ignatius. "In effect he teaches what Ouspensky taught, that we live our life—not lives—over and over again, and that it never varies. And yet the daring suggestion is added that it is possible to escape from this spiral of continual experience, that it is possible for one to be freed from this squirrel's cage by the intervention of some independent observer of the events of one's life."

"It's a form of soteria, of salvation," said Grayson. "And your dilemma, Brother?"

"I am supposed to refrain from intervening in the life of anyone unless specifically requested to do so."

The little priest sighed. "I have sometimes failed."

"If you saw a man plunging from a bridge into a river—committing suicide?"

"It is his own life, and he is solely responsible for what he does with it."

The little priest spoke as if reciting from a rule book. It was fairly obvious to Grayson that he did not believe what he was saying.

Grayson eyed him thoughtfully for a few moments. "And yet I've heard your name mentioned in murder cases, coupled with the name of that fellow from the Yard."

"Gordon Knollis."

"Knollis," said Grayson.

"Coupled would hardly be the word my friend Gordon would like you to use. I am his antithesis. He works on his cases to seek out the guilty . . ."

"And you?"

"To protect the innocent."

"But hang it . . . !" protested Grayson.

Brother Ignatius shook his head. "They are not the same thing at all, Mr. Grayson. Now if I had your permission to discuss your recent misfortunes . . ."

Grayson gave a wry grin. "Everybody else seems to have had a go at them, so I don't see why you should hesitate."

"Two years ago you went into partnership with Graham Dickinson. You had a more than fairish reputation as a writer of novels of detection—irrespective of the opinion of your relatives, and were well known for countryside stories written under a *nom de plume*. Dickinson was—and still is—a more than fairish satirist, essayist, and reviewer. He conceived the idea of a monthly magazine that should do something to bring town and country together. Between you, you were to take the town to the countryman, and the country to the townsman.

"Eighteen months ago you published the first number. It was good, very good, and I hope you will not think my praise to be in any way patronising. Nevertheless, the seeds of its own destruction were born with it. Your styles were so different! Dickinson's slick and sophisticated satirical sketches. Your own steady, and to the townman, plodding manner. It was like expecting a race horse and—and—"

"A race horse and a plough horse to work together in double harness," suggested Grayson. "I couldn't agree more. It was a darned good idea that just could not work. Heigh-ho!"

"But even after a year, when you realised that the venture was doomed, you refused to cut your losses and get out, if you will allow the colloquialism. The house in which you lived in St. John's Wood was your own, and you raised money on it in an attempt to keep the magazine alive. You stuck by your friend, and went down with him."

"Down to the bottom of the deep blue sea," said Grayson. "Every bloody thing went—sorry, Brother! Three weeks ago the furniture, and the household lares and penates went into storage for an indeterminate time. We got out just one jump ahead of the sheriff. My wife and child are staying temporarily with my not-so-beloved brother-in-law and his wife, my wife's sister, while Failure stays on in a bed-sitter in Kensington and tries to rebuild my family's fortunes.

"Once a week I travel by this train to Wingford to see 'em both, and hitchhike back on Sunday nights while they all attend evensong at the little church round the corner, the church of Our Lady and All Saints—which should be renamed Santa Maria della Grazie. They all pray for me—they say, but my brother-in-law's prayers have not been answered. I remain in excellent health."

"Your brother-in-law took them into his house," Brother Ignatius reminded him.

"For the same reason that he, and so many other self-styled Christians attend church; for it is seemly so to do. I prefer the man who gives his alms secretly, and prays to the Father in the privacy of his own closet."

"Nevertheless, he gave them a home."

"He came over to London, nattered at me like John Knox abjuring the ladies and gentlemen of the court circle to refrain from adultery, and said he could find room for Corinne and Natalie. There wasn't room for me, since Wingford Manor has only seventeen rooms. Not that I wanted to go. In the eyes of the world I had dropped a clanger, and I'd done it in London, and I wanted to stay on the battleground of my defeat and prove myself in my own environment—meeting the same critics every day and smiling through them in the safe knowledge that I could and would pull the game straight and scoop the kitty. You think I was ungrateful to Herby? In an ungracious way I was very grateful to him, and the roof he offered them. Natalie is enjoying the village school, and Corinne is—I hope—having a chance to think things over. At the moment I cannot count her as an active member of my fan club."

"And if anyone should suggest helping you?" queried Brother Ignatius.

"Firstly I should be vastly surprised, and secondly I should probably tell them to go to the devil," Grayson replied frankly.

"Preferring to stay in the suffocating vortex of eternal recurrence? Preferring to live the same confounding life over and over again—experiencing the same frustrations, the same sorrows?"

Grayson stared hard into the bowl of his pipe. "I'm more with Lahsen than Ouspensky. I'm inclined to believe that experience is only repeated until we have learned the lessons entailed in it. Once that is done, the experience is no longer repeated, and we move on to the next class. Candidly, I don't think outside intervention can possibly help. The responsibility is ours as individuals. Didn't the Buddha, from his death-bed, warn his favourite disciple that each man must work out his own salvation?"

"Intervention can be a risky procedure," Brother Ignatius agreed.

"It can also offend the man who wants to put his own life to rights off his own bat."

"Yet you allowed your brother-in-law to intervene!"

"I let him intervene in the lives of Corinne and Natalie—mainly for the child's sake," said Grayson. "If he tries to go further than that I'll kick his fat behind—"

"What do you know of his background?"

"He was managing director of three small collieries in Lancashire that paid decent dividends only by paying indecent wages in defiance of the men's union. After Vesting Day, and he was paid out by the State, he was well and truly in the money. He asked a London agent to find him a place in the eastern counties, far from the scene of his depredations. It was on the market because John Vere Bolding couldn't keep pace with taxation. Herby got it for a song, and ever since he's tried his damnedest to be the squire—but the 'yokels' as he calls them won't wear him.

"He's sent out invitations to the gentry to join him at dinner, and he and Gwen have had the board to themselves. He's fished for incoming invitations, and can't get the fish even to smell the bait. No, Brother, he bought himself a prison of Jacobean stone walls, mullioned windows, and hedges of *cupressus macrocarpa*. In some ways I'm sorry for him. He can't read. He has no appreciation of music. He doesn't know the difference between a Turner and a cow-cake calendar, and if you offered him a bust of Chopin and one of Popeye he wouldn't know which one was made for striking matches on. Poor devil!"

"A case, if ever there was one, for intervention," murmured Brother Ignatius.

"May the old gentleman with the scythe oblige," said Grayson with mock piety.

"He doesn't like you?"

"There are *two* very full ears," said Brother Ignatius. He lowered his feet from the opposite seat and briskly rubbed his stiffened knees. "You have something to read?"

"That most soothing and consoling work by John Cowper Powys, *The Philosophy of Solitude.*"

"In which case, if you will pardon me, I will return to my Lahsen."

"May heaven grant you the grace of enlightenment," said Grayson.

Brother Ignatius bowed his head. "You also, Mr. Grayson."

Grayson re-lit his pipe and buried himself in the chapter devoted to the problem of the self at bay, but for some considerable time the little priest continued to look up from the pages of Lahsen's volume with troubled and compassionate eyes, as if some knowledge of what the future held for his travelling companion was within him, and as if he was afraid, but not for himself.

II
Prelude to Battle

TWO WRITERS lived in Wingford village. Paul Longcroft described himself facetiously as a purveyor of commercial fiction to the proletariat, lived alone in a cottage behind the church, and was "done for "by old Mrs. Walters. Michael Costock was the author of two highly literary novels, several slim volumes of modern verse, and the daily menus of the Barley Mow, of which he was mine host.

Both were well known to Grayson, both were in when he sauntered through the doorway to the bar parlour, and both nodded just too carelessly as he greeted them. Both knew his story, understood the code that had ordered his own destruction, and at all times, in accordance with the tenets of that code, avoided mentioning the matter. Grayson knew that they knew, knew that they understood even if they did not agree, and was grateful for their silence. He waved towards the two near-empty glasses on the counter, and said: "Fill 'em up, Mike."

Costock, a handsome, black-haired man of thirty-five, Grayson's own age, fulfilled his duties as landlord, and without any explanation to Grayson continued an argument with Longcroft.

"And as I was saying when I was interrupted by this gentleman from London, you are no more than a literary prostitute."

Longcroft, an untidy individual of forty-three who had chosen a red bow tie and an ancient and once bright green beret as the main items of relief against a faded and patched heather tweed suit, grinned broadly at Grayson.

"The only differences between the prostitute and the courtesan," he said, "are the amount of window dressing and the prices charged. I'd drown myself sooner than write the trash you've foisted across an unintelligent public—and if I've said that once in this pub I must have said it fifty times. Your stuff says nothing, means nothing, and does nothing. Niente, niente, niente! Or as the French have it, sweet fanny adams!"

Costock folded his arms on the edge of the bar counter, and pushed his aquiline nose into Longcroft's near-Cockney features.

"My stuff symbolises the stirrings of an ever-waking consciousness!"

"Pfft!" said Longcroft. "It reads like the constant stirrings of an undigested lobster. My writing may not be 'igh clarss, but by God it does tell stories!"

Costock nodded heavily. "It does! It does! It tells stories of the rape of the innocent, of a man who tries to make innocent working girls believe that Prince Charming is waiting just round the corner to whip them off to the altar and the bright lights. Your tripe makes them dissatisfied with life, and even when they marry some good and honest craftsman they lie in his arms and dream he's Prince Diarmid ben Sahara, or some other fictitious romantic clot of your imaginings."

"What's it matter so long as the boy friend's happy with what he's got?" asked Longcroft.

Grayson waited more or less patiently.

"Costock," he said at last. "A cupper tea, a wash, and a room, for the love of Allah!"

"Will you never learn?" Longcroft asked sadly. "Why not go down the road and lodge with the Armstrong family. They are not heretics as they are here, but God-fearing people. In your bedroom you'll find the Good Book and a copy of poems by Ella Wheeler Wilcox, and a very interesting agricultural implement catalogue in the toilet. And here? In this Godless house? In this wine-bibbers' rendezvous? Nothing on your bedside table but two volumes of perfumed slosh by Michael Costock, thrice past-president of the Universal Poetry Society."

Costock swung open the small door in the bar and jerked a thumb kitchenwards. "You know your own room, and the geography of the house—"

Said Longcroft softly: "The only place you won't find Costock's wonder writings is in the smallest room in the house, which is where it should be—hanging from a hook!" Costock flashed him a mock savage glance, and called out: "Doreen! Bran's arrived, and faint for tea."

He turned to Grayson. "Now leave me, friend, while I lash this Philistine with my tongue."

A dark vivacious woman three years younger than her husband hurried into view, grasped Grayson's hands in her own, and pulled him to her. "Darling! I'm so glad you've come again. Nat was here to see me yesterday. She's a sweet, sweet child!"

She looked up into his face.

"What's wrong, Bran, dear?"

Grayson screwed up his eyes as if to try and recollect something. "I don't know, Reen. I just don't know. It was just as if a cloud had passed over the moon. What a damn silly expression! I neither think nor write like that. Oh, well!"

Costock patted him on the shoulder. "You're tired, boy! Get the dust and smoke washed from your skin, and after a few cups of Doreen's tea you'll feel a new man."

"I guess you're right," said Grayson. Doreen Costock dropped his hands, and he went up the white-painted stairs to his room under the thatched eaves.

It was the room he had chosen for himself when he first came three weeks ago. Costock, a man of acute sensibilities, had shown him round the house, never pressing him for a choice, and allowed him to decide for himself to use the one room in the whole house from which he could see the manor, quarter of a mile away to the north of the village.

Since then the room had been kept ready for his coming by night or by day, and never a word said about it between a man and his wife who understood each other.

Grayson pushed open the stained plank door, and threw his rucksack and Burberry into a corner. He sat on the bed and took off his shoes; then went to the open casement and stared out across the fields.

Wingford Manor was Jacobean, a grey stone and delightful place, famous for its long and sombre yew walks and first-class topiary work. When John Vere Bolding was lord of the manor the gardens were open to the villagers all day and every day, and twice a year they were thrown open to the general public at a charge which benefited the cottage hospital at Yeagrave, the town four miles away. Moston had tried desperately to follow in the Vere Bolding tradition, but no villagers went near the gardens. They passed the wrought-iron gates only if they had business, and essential business, at the manor.

The gable window on the south wall of the east wing, the tiny dark patch he could see through a gap in the massed cypresses, was Natalie's room. Corinne's room lay behind it.

Grayson ran frenzied hands through his stubbled brown hair. God, it was like watching one's beloveds in a concentration camp from which there was no chance of escape! To see them once a week, almost on sufferance, and spend the rest of one's hours in exile, working and working to earn the ransom!

He closed his fists and brought them down again and again on the white sill. "Damn Herby, and damn Dickinson, and Brother Ignatius, and Lahsen, and the—"

Two hands clamped on his shoulders from behind and shook him vigorously. "Shut up, you fool! Do you want the whole village to know your heart!"

Costock swung him round, and pushed him hard against the mullion. "You poor devil!"

Grayson took a deep breath, and let it go in a long sobbing gasp. "Sorry, Mike! Three weeks, and it's the first time I've let go . . . I'm sorry."

Costock backed to the bed, sat on it, and crossed his legs. "Letting go's the right thing, old boy, but you're doing it the wrong way. You should learn to unstring the bow. You've left it strung, and now find a masochistic pleasure in twanging its nerves. The justices themselves know this is a temperate house, but if I don't get you sozzled before you go back to London you can call me Paul Longcroft—and may the gods preserve me from such a fate!"

"There's no longer any pleasure in drink, Mike."

"The death wish has crept into your subconscious," Costock said gently. "What are you doing about sleep?"

"Barbiturates."

"The death of each day's life, fair labour's bath," quoted Costock. "Only it isn't fair labour's bath in your case. It's just the welcome death of each day's life—a nightly substitute for final suicide. You are all right for just so long as you are writing. It's when you have time to think that it hurts. The deathly sleep is then welcome."

Grayson nodded his agreement. "Very welcome, Mike. I wake heavily, but with no dreams behind me."

"How's the book going?"

"Two-thirds through."

"What advance will you get?"

"Probably two-fifty."

"And then?"

"I can start to look for a house to buy on mortgage. Until then, you just can't rent a house or flat in town for that or less."

"Why stay in town—as if I didn't know the answer before I asked the question."

Grayson gave a twisted smile. "They laughed when I sat down to play . . ."

"And, being pig-headed, you have to show them that you really can play, and in their own drawing-room!"

"That's it, Mike!"

"Move in here with me and Doreen. You can see them every day then."

"Wouldn't work," Grayson said shortly. "Corinne was one of those who laughed after the piano stool collapsed, and I began to pick myself up. Apart from which, all the village would know we were receiving your gracious charity."

"Let me lend you the two-fifty, and start looking for a place in the suburbs as soon as you get back."

"I finish this book first," said Grayson. "Apart from which—again, Corinne will stand for no borrowing. She'll play for a mortgage once I've proved that I can still write to earn, and I have to stick to my last."

"Women," Costock said slowly, "pray o' Sundays to the Almighty, the Lord God of Hosts. From Monday to Saturday they lay their secret offerings at the feet of the idol called Security."

He stood up and clapped Grayson on the back. "Go and get a soaking bath. You'll find bath salts in the cupboard. I'll bring a cup of tea to the bathroom for you."

"Guess I made an ass of myself, Mike," said Grayson wryly. "I guess I eased the latch on the door of my emotions on the way down. Spent an hour or more nattering philosophy with a little priest who was visiting the village."

"Short chap? Lithe and lean? A black-frocked bloke wearing a skull-cap, and buckled shoes, and carrying a thumb-staff?"

"Name of Brother Ignatius, and a learned little man with a great fund of experience I should say."

Costock's tongue wandered over his lips. "Now I wonder what he's doing in Wingford?"

Grayson shrugged. "Does it matter? He said he was visiting a member of his flock, old Mrs. Walters."

"He's a queer little cuss," said Costock. "Nestorian, if that means anything to you-—which it doesn't to me. His flock appears to be spread over the earth from Baffin Bay to Cape Horn, and Vancouver Island to the Persian Gulf. I don't know the first thing about his sect, or denomination, or whatever you call it, but he seems to be a sort of peripatetic monk or friar or something. He's either got psychic powers, or a first-rate M.I.5 organisation working for him, because he always turns up—"

He broke off abruptly. "That's Doreen mounting the stairs with a cupper. Like her to serve it to you in the bath?"

The deliberately lascivious leer on Costock's face brought a smile to Grayson's harassed features. "Her husband might object," he said.

"How right," said Costock.

Grayson did not go through the village to the manor house until after tea. He was under an obligation to Herby as it was, an obligation of which he was reminded on every visit, and apart from wanting to see Herby as little as possible while wanting to see Corinne and Natalie as often as possible, he realised that for the comfort of his wife and child he had to tread warily.

While still two hundred yards from the manor he heard a shrill "Coo-ee-ee!" and answered it. There came the patter of running feet, and Natalie threw herself into his arms with a tremulous "My big daddy!"

Natalie was nearly eight, a dark-haired, dark-eyed elfin child so much like her mother that Grayson winced at the sight of her even as he kissed her, and for a short second expected her to start pitching into him for landing them in this mess instead of letting Dickinson go to the devil alone. Then it was gone, and hand in hand they were chasing along the pink-gravelled road to where Corinne waited by one of the lion-crowned stone gate-posts.

"Hello, dear!" he said.

Corinne glanced at Natalie, and forced a welcoming smile. "She's been asking for you all day," she said.

"How's things?" asked Grayson, and was aware of the banality of the question.

"Comme ci comme ça," she replied with a Gallic movement of her hands. In French she said quickly: "The uncle of the child is gunning for the father of the child." Grayson sighed. "That's been the case for many years, my dear. What you can't under-

stand, you fear. And what you fear, you kill. What's the nature of the material up the spout?"

"I don't know, but he's looking particularly pleased with himself."

"Gobble," said Grayson.

"What's the spout?" asked Natalie.

Quick glances were exchanged by husband and wife.

"It's just a saying, darling," Corinne replied. Her lip achieved a momentary and sarcastic twist. "One of Daddy's funny sayings."

Natalie grasped his hand and danced round him. "Daddy has lots and lots of funny sayings, hasn't he?"

"He most certainly has," Corinne said dryly.

They dawdled up the yew-lined drive to the house. "Going to show your face, Bran?"

Grayson nodded. "I suppose I'd better."

"Why is Daddy going to show his face, Mummy?" Corinne looked at her husband for the answer.

"To prove that I shaved before I came out this morning, my sweet!"

The child was delighted with the answer, and demanded to be picked up so that she could feel the smoothness of his cheeks. Then she slid through his arms to the ground, and ran ahead into the entrance hall, calling out to her uncle.

"Uncle Herbert! Daddy's going to show you his face, to prove that he's shaved!"

Grayson and Corinne followed her through to the morning room, where Moston was spread out full length in a deep fire-side chair of unknown parentage.

"I know that, Nat," he said without looking up. "Your daddy always was bare-faced."

"Evening, Herbert," said Grayson. "I trust I see you well?"

Moston eased his bulk from the chair, and eyed Grayson with extreme distaste. He remarked that it all depended on the state of his eyes.

He was a man of something over forty, a well-made man, which Grayson had to admit in spite of all his prejudice. He was tending to over-plumpness through lack of exercise, but looked good for another thirty or more years, a fact which Grayson regretted. It was his eyes that always interested Grayson. They were practically lacking pigment; pale, expressionless, fish-like eyes behind which there might be much—or nothing. And Grayson could never decide which.

Remembering Corinne's warning, he looked Moston over cautiously. They lived in entirely different worlds, and neither understood the other. Both were continually on the watch lest the other should jump a claim. Grayson was also aware that if Herby could widen the rift between Corinne and himself he would do so. He had tried to stop Corinne marrying him those ten years ago, and was now in an excellent position to make up for lost time.

They stared at each other coolly for a time, and then Moston turned away to take a cigarette from a cheap but ornamental box on the mantelpiece and light it with an expensive lighter.

Grayson had no difficulty in recognising the insolent mode of dismissal, and followed Corinne down the oak-floored corridors to the lounge, where Natalie still grasping his hand tightly and dancing along beside him.

"Anything to talk about?" he asked Corinne when they were alone.

"I think everything's been said that can be said," she replied. "How are things in town? How's the book coming along?"

"Hawkes has seen the synopsis and the first five chapters, and is prepared to advance two-fifty on receipt of the manuscript."

"How long will it take you?"

"Another fortnight. I'm doing ten to twelve thousand a day—which is ruinous to my style."

"That means you're staying up at night?"

"No. No, not exactly," said Grayson. "Meals make it a wee bit difficult, so I'm breaking up the writing time. An hour before breakfast, which I cook for myself. Two hours before lunch, which I take at the cafe round the corner. Revision and correction until tea, which I also prepare myself, and then two and a half hours in the evening. Coffee and rolls, or toast, at the cafe round about ten o'clock, and then work until one. Broken up like that it comes easy."

"Don't go and work yourself out as you have before," Corinne said.

Grayson raised one of his heavy eyebrows. She had said it flatly, without any feeling. It was a conventional remark, straight from a last-century volume on how to be the complete conversationalist.

He stirred uneasily, and to avoid her eyes looked through the mullioned window to the Peacock Lawn, and the tall cypresses beyond. Symbolically, clouds were gathering, and the world outside was deathly still.

Natalie broke the silence. "Oo! I've something to show you! Mummy bought me a lovely book in Yeagrave. I'll fetch it from my room."

As she scampered away Corinne walked into the window, and stood with her back towards him. The room was cold, and Grayson uncertain of himself. He took a half-step towards his wife, and then stopped.

The quietness of the room was a tangible thing, something that could be felt. It wrapped itself round him, pressed tightly to his body. The only sound was a far distant murmur of thunder, and the rapid ticking of the French travelling clock on the white marble mantelshelf, hurrying on as if wishing to reach the end of time and be free of its labours.

The oversized porcelain knob on the white door turned, and Natalie came in, hugging her new book.

"You'd better look at it later, Daddy," she said solemnly. "Uncle says he wants to talk to you straight away. He's going to wait for you on Peacock."

"So it's here," Grayson said soberly. "I'd better go and get it over."

"You'll come and say goodnight to me, Daddy?"

"I'll come and say goodnight to you, darling," said Grayson.

Corinne remained in the window, motionless.

III
Sentence of Exile

MOSTON WAS STROLLING importantly up and down the Peacock Lawn, his fingers inside and his thumbs outside his jacket pockets. His chin was elevated, and his eyes fixed on the far distance as if staring into one of Ouspensky's many dimensions. Grayson could imagine him in the days before nationalisation, walking up and down his office as he dictated the details of a new policy to a long-suffering secretary. He knew that on this occasion the new policy concerned himself.

"The above has arrived," Grayson announced, and winced as a whiplash of lightning cleaved the sky. He put on a relaxed and detached smile for Herby's benefit, and started to polish the bowl of his pipe on the ball of his thumb.

"I've been thinking," Moston said pontifically.

Grayson was about to congratulate him on a rare event, but changed his mind, and decided to hear him out.

"There's something about you that I've never liked, Grayson," Moston continued.

Grayson put his head askew to indicate that he was interested. He also tapped his teeth with the stem of his pipe, and kept his eyes focused on the bridge of Moston's nose with the intention of intimidating him with the continued stare.

"I knew Corinne was making a mistake when she married you," went on Moston. "I did my best to prevent her marrying you."

"I'd be honest, and call it your worst," said Grayson. "You certainly made life a hell for us both until we *were* married, and she was out of your reach."

Moston bowed his head in acknowledgment of the fact. "And you've made it hell for her ever since."

"You're wrong there, Herby," Grayson said earnestly. "Life was great fun for us both until a year ago. Since then it's been hell for us both, and got worse since she came here with Nat."

"And who did she come to when she was in trouble?" demanded Moston belligerently.

Grayson continued to stare at the root of Moston's nose, and played the stem of the pipe across his chin.

"There's something in law books about benefactors to wives being in good fortune when they make their offers, and about husbands being in bad fortune when their wives are removed from them," he said. "It comes in the sections devoted to incitement and abduction cases, and has to do with such situations as the present one. You should read it up some time."

"She came to me," said Moston.

"You're a liar," Grayson replied without passion. "You came to her, in London, because you saw the chance for which you had waited many years."

"To take her away from a worthless scamp—a—a writer! You were never content to earn an honest living like I've done—"

"Good God!" Grayson ejaculated, in genuine amazement.

"You wanted to be a gentleman, and you've brought your wife to poverty, and lost the house which was Natalie's heritage. You've also shamed me and Gwen."

"You mean you've lost face at second hand," said Grayson. "As for losing Nat's heritage, I'd sooner do that through over-honesty than have Wingford the way you got it."

Moston took a step towards him, and then paused as he looked into Grayson's eyes. "Why, you . . ."

"Get it over, Herby," Grayson said softly. "The script was written ages ago. You've lain in bed o' nights thinking it out, with many melodramatic details which you daren't add now we're face to face. Get it over, Herby. You should know it by heart!"

"I've—I've waited for years for this chance," Moston said savagely, "and now you can have it. Corinne and Natalie can stay under my protection as long as they like, but after tonight I never want to see you on these premises again. When you get out tonight you stay out!"

"No more doorstep darkening, eh?" murmured Grayson. "Y'know, Herby, you do it quite well to say how short of guts you really are. If I could play a violin I'd strum *Hearts and Flowers* as background music."

"I don't pretend to understand that," said Moston. "In some ways you're cleverer than me. You've written mystery novels which have kept me guessing right to the last page-"

"*Et tu, Brute?*" said Grayson.

"Yes, kept me guessing. If you can do that in a book you might be clever enough to do it in real life. I don't know what's in your mind about Corinne and Natalie and yourself, and I'm not taking any risks. So get out and stay out."

Grayson nodded, and stowed the pipe in his pocket.

"Okay, Herby! They are your preserves, and I'm the one in the jam who doesn't even get tuppence on the jar. I take it I have your gracious permission to re-enter the house on this notable occasion to say goodnight to Natalie? She's in bed by now."

"You have my permission," Moston said gravely.

Grayson bowed from the waist, muttered his thanks, and went back to the house as lightning played across the sky and the murmurs and rumbles grew nearer.

He met Corinne on the corridor, just coming from Natalie's room.

"Did you know this was going to happen?" he asked. "You said Herby had something in mind, but did you know what it was?"

Her face was cold, almost carved. "Whatever has happened, I knew nothing of it. Neither did Gwen."

"Herby's slung me out. Made a real Tod Slaughter job of it, too. It was only by inches he missed telling me not to darken his threshold again."

"Well?" Corinne demanded icily. "What did you expect him to do?"

Grayson blinked. "What did you say, darling?"

"Don't darling me!"

He moved to take her in his arms, but she stiffened her body against him, and turned her head to avoid his lips.

"Corinne!"

"Say goodnight to Natalie, and I'll go with you to the bottom of the drive."

"Yes, you must," said Grayson. "Herby has no dogs to see me off."

He pushed open the bedroom door as a great peal of thunder rumbled over the house. Natalie, never afraid of storms, was pretending to be fast asleep, but an impish smile played round her dimpled cheeks.

Grayson tiptoed to the bed, and leaned over the old-gold sheets and the matching pillow and coverlet.

"So Prince Charming bent over the Princess and woke her with a kiss, and they lived happily ever after."

Natalie bounced up in bed, and as she looked up at him her smile faded. Grayson knelt beside her and put his head against her smooth cheek. "Princess, do you love your daddy?"

"You, and Mummy, and Auntie Gwen. Uncle Herby isn't nice, is he?"

"You mustn't say such things, darling. We are all children of God."

"He's sending you away from us, isn't he?"

Grayson drew away to look into her solemn eyes.

"Now how would you know that?" he asked gently.

"I listened behind the curtains while Mummy was in the bathroom."

"Does she know you listened, Nat?"

The little head rocked to and fro in a definite negative.

"Then please don't tell her that you know. It would make her unhappy."

"But she'll *know* you're not coming back!"

"Yes," said Grayson, "she'll know, but she wouldn't like to think that you know. She'll make excuses to you about me being very busy in London on the book, and things like that. It isn't supposed to be good for little girls to know much about grown-up troubles."

"I—I hate him, Daddy!" she exclaimed with childish fervour.

Grayson glanced quickly at her, and hesitated.

"Well," he said uncertainly, "I can't say what I should say to you. I should tell you it's all wrong to hate anybody—anybody at all, but I've always tried to be honest with you, and I'm blessed if I'm going to be a hypocrite and tell you to try to love him."

"What's a hypo—you know!"

"It's a person who says one thing while he thinks just the opposite, Nat."

"Like when Herby pats me on the head and says he loves me as if I was his own?"

"I think that's just it, young 'un," said Grayson, and turned his eyes up to heaven in a silent prayer for the protection of his child.

"Daddy!"

"Mm?"

"What's different values? Mummy said it once to you when you were quarrelling in London, and she said it to Herby yesterday when he was 'on' about you."

He glanced askew at her, and scratched his head.

"Y'know, your generation are one up on mine—and you won't understand that, either. What are different values, eh? Now there's a question if ever there was one. Your mother would play pop with me if she knew we were talking like this, but it may be some time before we're together again, and what I'm going to say may help you."

Natalie edged nearer to him, and laid an arm across his shoulders.

"It's like this," said Grayson slowly, feeling his way into an explanation that she could understand. "It's like this, Nat. Your mummy and me love beautiful pictures because they are beautiful, and good books because they tell of good things, and we like flowers because they are pretty, and smell nice, and help to make the world a nice place to live in. Herby doesn't see things that way at all, so we and he have different values . . .

"He only likes things because of what they cost. A picture is a good one to him if it has cost him a lot of money, and not because it is beautiful. I'm telling you this for one reason only. Not to make you hate Herby any more than you do, but so that you'll grow up to love things for their real value—because they are good, and beautiful, and true. There's one other thing, sweetheart. Herby thinks he's doing the best for you and mummy because I think more about books, and pictures, and flowers, and nice things generally than I do about having more money than I can spend. Anyway, it won't be so very long before we are all together again, and just as you aren't afraid of lightning and thunder, so you must not be afraid of this rather nasty time. You've got to be brave just a wee bit longer, and look after mummy for me."

He hugged her to him.

"And now it's goodnight, Princess. I'll see you again very soon—not here, of course, but somewhere, and I'll write to you every day."

The tiny arms crept round his neck. Wet eyes were pushed hard against his cheek, and the sobbing grew to heartbroken gasps. Grayson choked back a sob of his own, laid her down in the bed, tucked the soft arms under the coverlet, and kissed her gently on the mouth. Then he hurried from the room, not daring to look back at the tiny sobbing figure in the golden bed.

Corinne and Moston were in the lounge when he got downstairs. Gwen was with them, a younger version of Corinne, with the same dark hair but more calculating eyes. The three stood in a protective group on the hearth.

Grayson paused in the doorway, partly for dramatic effect, and looked them over with a wry and bitter smile before striding across to Moston's bearskin hearthrug.

"Herby," he said, "I don't need to go melodramatic over this action of yours. I leave such antics to uncultured people like yourself who can only be noticed by striking a pose. I don't need to talk any nonsense about getting my own back, either. Life is run by laws, and among them is the law of compensation. The ball thrown against a wall comes back to you. The beam of light flung at a mirror is reflected to its source—and the angle of reflection is equal to the angle of incidence. You won't understand all that, any more than any one of the three of you can really understand why I live my life the way I do."

He paused, and winced as the lightning played across the white mantel.

"I try to live to a code. Sometimes I find it difficult. At the moment I can feel more pity for you than anger—"

"You've nothing to pity me for!" exclaimed Moston angrily.

"Oh, but I have," said Grayson. "True ignorance is the state of not knowing what you don't know—and there's so much in your case. But what I was going to say was that I don't feel violent towards you, not at the moment, but I don't trust you as far as I could blow you, and so I want to warn you quite fairly, and in front of witnesses, that if you make the slightest attempt to come between Natalie and myself I shan't just beat you up—I shall kill you, and you'll die hard!"

He turned to Corinne. "You said you'd walk down the drive with me!"

Moston put out a detaining hand. "You're not safe with him!"

Grayson took a step forward, and Moston took one back. "Be careful, Herby! You're the only person in this house in peril—and by God you don't know how near you are to death!"

Corinne marched from Moston's side, and stiff-limbed accompanied him between the tall yew hedges to the gates, oblivious of the incessant thunder and the late evening sky now continually criss-crossed with red flashes until it looked like a fiery gridiron.

"It isn't going to rain, you know," said Grayson. "I once saw a storm like this in the Med—southern Greece it was to be accurate. Lasted three days and three nights, and nary a drop of rain."

Corinne passed no comment, and at last they came to the Lion Gates.

"So it's heigh-ho for the Barley Mow," said Grayson. "When and how and where do I see you again?"

"You make the arrangements, and I'll keep them so that you can see Natalie."

"Why phrase it that way?" Grayson asked.

She pushed her face fiercely into his. "Haven't you realised that it's all over?"

"Well, yes. People will talk. You can't stop them."

"I mean it's all over between us—between you and me!"

Grayson dropped his hands on her shoulders. "What the hell are you talking about, darling?"

"Take your hands from my shoulders, please!"

He did so, and peered at her through the eerie light of the electric storm, but still not understanding.

"Where were we? I'm lost," he said.

"I'm not coming back to you, not as your wife."

She said it flatly, unemotionally.

Grayson almost giggled at the absurdity of the remark.

"Don't be so damn silly, Corinne," he said. "You're catching Herby's Victorianism."

In a quick voice she said: "You must get us a home together as soon as you can, for Natalie's sake. I shall come back to you, but not as your wife. We shall keep up the pretence for her sake. I shall keep house for you, and help to provide a home for the three of us, but that is all."

Grayson said nothing. There was a peculiar numbness creeping over his brain, a kind of caul that seemed to have been folded at the nape of his neck and was now being drawn upwards and over his head, but inside his skull, like a blind. It crept over his forehead . . .

The whole thing was a stupid, unreal, and illogical dream. Corinne was not coming back, not as his wife. She would keep house for him. She would keep up the pretence of marriage for the sake of Natalie. She . . .

"Corinne!" he said slowly, and groped for her like a sightless man. Then he realised that she was not with him. She had gone, and he had not seen her go.

The merciful blind pressed down on his cerebral cortex until he was not even aware of existence. When the pressure lifted he was standing in the smoke room of the inn, a pint tankard of beer in his hand. Costock was lolling on the jamb of the serving hatch, watching him steadily.

Grayson forced himself to speak. "Hello, old boy!"

"Hello, Bran," said Costock. He withdrew, and busied himself with the tap-room clientele on the other side of the wall.

Grayson found his tankard empty, and walked across the room to put it on the wide shelf of the half-door. Some time later he noticed that he was leaning against the fireplace, and the tankard was again empty-—either that, or he had forgotten to get it refilled. He took it across to the half-door.

Still later, Harry Vere Bolding came in, gave his order to Costock, glanced curiously at Grayson, and gently relieved him of the tankard in order to have it filled.

Grayson nodded gratefully. Vere Bolding was a decent fellow, a gentleman farmer with something like two thousand acres at his command; the brother of John Vere Bolding who had once owned the manor of Wingford. He was a dignified man approaching sixty, with thin grey hair, and who was seldom seen wearing any other suit but a patched one of ginger plus-fours, with which he wore a tweed hat. A countryman, and a gentleman.

He was followed in by Paul Longcroft, and it seemed to Grayson that the "tripe writer" as Costock called him to his face also stared at him curiously before Vere Bolding got him a drink. Then they both sat down, and continued to stare at him, albeit furtively.

Halfway down their pints they were joined by Henry Crewley, who had the estate of Wingford under his care. He was wont to say that he had the misfortune to be Mr. Moston's bailiff, and he said it to all and sundry without hesitation or care whether it got back to the manor or not. He was a lean, shrewd man of Yorkshire birth, and many years in the eastern counties had not ruined his accent, although he dropped into dialect only when strongly stirred or when telling smoke-room stories about the north.

"All right, Mr. Grayson?" he inquired politely.

Grayson nodded. He felt the need to sit down, but for some queer reason his body refused to obey orders, and so he remained standing, his weight taken on the corner of the fireplace.

"Wife and kiddy all right up there?"

Grayson looked across the room, and saw him only through a blue-grey mist apparently caused by the weight which pressed down on his brain and came down like a vee between his eyes.

He said something about Corinne, and was vaguely aware that Costock had come into the room, and was standing with his back against the closed door, almost as if to keep any newcomers out. Doreen was leaning through the hatch, resting her arms on the wide shelf of the half-door, listening.

Longcroft said something about Moston being the worst bastard he had ever met.

Grayson talked on and on. He paused only to glare into his empty tankard. Costock took it, handed it to Doreen, and returned it to Grayson filled. Grayson emptied it, and continued to talk. He tried to silence his tongue, and was unable to do so. He could not hear what he was saying, and that annoyed him.

The heaviness was increasing, too. It was spreading from his forehead to his eyelids, and all his efforts to keep them from falling over his eyes were useless. They were the masters.

And then, as the thunder rolled and rumbled and echoed overhead, the heaviness suddenly vanished, and the shroud lifted from his consciousness. He nodded affably to Vere Bolding. "My round, I think, Colonel."

"That's right," said Costock. "I wondered when you were going to pay your whack. Round the room, of course?"

"And you and Doreen, please."

He stroked his forehead. "Funny, that! Must have dozed off—standing up at that!"

"Warmth of the room, a heavy night, and little wind with this storm running round," said Longcroft.

"Damned queerest dream ever," said Grayson. "Herby had turfed me out of Wingford, and Corinne told me she wasn't coming back as my wife, and I told Herby I'd kill him if he—-"

He looked round the faces of the people watching him so strangely. Vere Bolding, Longcroft, Crewley, Mike Costock, and Doreen.

"Oh, my God!" he said, and sprawled across the floor on his face.

Longcroft was the first to speak. "Better get His Nibs into bed."

"No," said Costock. "I'm not taking him through the house in that state. The story would soon be round that he was drunk."

"Well? Isn't he?"

Costock shook his head. "A doctor would say he was suffering from shock. No, get him up on the settle behind the door, and watch him. Nobody else is likely to be in here tonight."

"Nervous shock," said Vere Bolding. "No wonder, poor devil!"

"But why all the secrecy?" demanded Longcroft. The understanding possessed by the others escaped him.

"You heard what he said?" asked Costock. "You heard his story?"

"Well, yes!"

Vere Bolding took over from Costock. "Can't you imagine the rejoicing at the manor house if it leaked out that Moston had given his brother-in-law the *coup-de-grâce*?"

"Ye-es," Longcroft said hesitantly. Then he added: "I wish to God I'd been educated like you chaps!"

"There's nothing wrong with you," said Costock. "Now up with him!"

They put him to bed after closing time, and there he stayed, despite many protestations, until early evening the next day. Tea was a late occasion on Sundays, and it was not until six o'clock that Doreen allowed him downstairs to a lightly-boiled egg, home-made wholemeal bread, and farm butter.

He said nothing about the previous night, because he was not at all sure about it. He knew that something abnormal had happened to him, but was not aware of its nature. Everyone around him seemed to be acting normally, and he put what little he could remember of his weird experience down to some circulatory disturbance which had produced the kind of out-of-this-world nightmare he had experienced some years before while under anaesthetic in an operating chamber—that was the time they took out his appendix.

The inn opened at seven, and after glancing through the notes for the next chapter he was due to write he went through to the smoke-room, taking his portfolio with him. Costock brought him a tankard of bitter beer without being asked, and returned to the bar.

Grayson concentrated on his notes for the first hour, when the regulars began to drift in at five-minute intervals; first Longcroft, then Crewley, and finally Vere Bolding. He put the portfolio behind him on the settle, and joined in the general sociability.

Longcroft wondered when this queer storm would finish, and Grayson realised that the thunder and lightning had continued without a break for twenty-four hours, and yet no rain had fallen.

"We had one like this when I was in Araxos, in the Peloponnese, during the last year of the war," said Grayson. "Never a drop of rain, but the air was so electric that little blue sparks were dancing on the wireless and V.H.F. masts all the time, and the way the lightning played round Mount Erymanthos reminded me of the old Greek legends of the gods at battle on Mount Olympus. Lasted three days, and the station was out of commission all that time."

"Not nice for the children," said Crewley. "We had to have our two in bed with us all last night. Looks like being the same tonight."

"Should be corn-ripening, shouldn't it?" asked Longcroft.

Crewley looked at him as if he had suggested that Thor and Vulcan were still at work in the world. Then, as if despising Longcroft's question he said: "Talking of children, I'll be glad when they're back at school. What with my own two whooping it up all the time, and bringing their chums to help them, the place is like Bedlam!"

"They're on holiday again this next week?" asked Grayson, suddenly interested in the conversation.

"All this next week!" Crewley said bitterly.

Grayson smiled to himself. Apart from the private telephone in the kitchen, at the other end of the house, there was a coin box for the use of patrons in the passage, just outside the smoke-room door.

He excused himself, and went to it, rammed threepence through the slot, and asked for the Wingford Manor number, Yeagrave 142. He left the door open, and the three men in the smoke-room listened shamelessly, and were joined by Costock, who listened through the hatch.

"That Alice? This is Mr. Grayson."

Alice Day was Moston's housemaid.

"Look, Alice; ask Mrs. Grayson if she can have Nat ready for ten o'clock in the morning, and waiting at the Lion Gates. I'd like to take her into Yeagrave for the day . . ."

His voice trailed away. He said "What" and "Yes" twice, and then silently replaced the handset and returned to the smoke-room.

"Something wrong?" asked Longcroft.

Grayson forced himself to look up from the floor. The heaviness was creeping over the crown of his skull again.

"According to Alice Day—and why should she lie to me? According to Alice, my young 'un told Herby what she thought of him this morning for sending me away from her. Herby went berserk, and apparently used some pretty bad language to her. Corinne went to the aid of her child—and what mother wouldn't do just that?—and Herby's slung them out. He doesn't care where they go, or whether they've anywhere to go or not. They have to get out before morning. Corinne hasn't bothered letting me know. She's phoned an aunt at Yarmouth, and is taking Nat there . . ."

He smiled at them. "You will excuse me? I have to go out."

"He's a big bloke," said Longcroft, as if talking to himself.

"While he was otherwise busy during the war," said Grayson, "I was marching up and down North Africa, Sicily, Italy, and a few places east of that. I was in three riots, one invasion, and the Greek uncivil war. The decencies and obscenities of unarmed combat were so well drilled into me that they became habits which tend to return to action when suitably stimulated."

Four pairs of eyes watched him walk purposefully from the room. Four pairs of ears listened as his footsteps retreated down the flagged passage, turned right, and clanked over the steel-grille mud-mat. They heard him plod firmly up the road, crunching over the gravel, and the apparently never-to-cease thunder murmured and rumbled round the old-world village.

Vere Bolding looked down at the table, and gave a little cough. "If you fellows will excuse me for a little while . . . ? I forgot to make a call on the way down. Rather important, y'know!"

He left his drink unfinished.

Crewley gave a short and uncertain laugh. "Poor old Grayson's troubles seem to be affecting us all the same way. I promised to call and see old Ball about his roof. Might be serious if rain does come. Picturesque, these old stone cottages, but once you get a stone roof cracked it's Old Harry himself keeping the damp out."

"And that left two," murmured Costock. "Another on the house, my Philistinic friend?"

Longcroft shook his head. "No, thanks. We shan't get a game of dominoes until the gang re-assemble, so I think I'll dodge back to finish off another yard of tripe ready for the morning collection. I'll probably pop back later."

"Do! Oh, do!" said Costock.

When Longcroft had gone he took off his white apron, and went through to the kitchen for his coat and cap. "Look after the bar for a while, Reen," he said. "I've been called out on a spot of business. One of our friends in trouble—y'know!"

Doreen merely nodded. She was accustomed to stepping in while her husband performed secret acts of charity. He would—and did—go miles to help anyone in trouble. It was one of the many reasons why she loved him so much.

IV
Herald of Misfortune

IT WAS AN hour and a half later when Grayson walked back into the smoke-room, looking smugly pleased with himself. There was nothing to indicate that the room had been empty for an hour of the time he had been away. Vere Bolding, Crewley, and

Longcroft were playing a version of five-and-threes on the dominoes table in the corner, and Costock was trying to cope with both sides of the bar in the remaining quarter of an hour before closing time. Grayson nodded affably all round, and then blinked his surprise as he noticed Brother Ignatius sitting behind the wooden draught wing attached to the settle immediately inside the door. It was not that he was surprised at seeing a priest in a pub, but he had a pint glass in front of him on the table, and the beer had almost reached refillment stage.

"Good evening, Brother!" he said.

"To you, also, Mr. Grayson. You seem surprised to see me— or to see me here. You will allow me to offer you a drink?"

"Er—well, thanks," said Grayson.

Brother Ignatius twirled the knob of the bell, and when Costock came in he waved a hand round the room.

"All of them. Why not take all of them," crooned Costock. He looked at Grayson and wrinkled his nose. "Pleased as a pussy with a bowl of cream, Bran. Why-fore?"

"Knuckles of your right hand are bleeding, cock!" said Longcroft.

"Unrighteous blood spilt in a righteous cause," said Grayson happily. "I went up and clocked Herby, and I guess he has something to think about now."

Harry Vere Bolding laid his dominoes on the table. "You did—what?"

"Clocked him! Hit him! Laid him low in the dust of his own gun-room floor!"

Brother Ignatius touched him gently on the arm. "I know I should suppress my curiosity, but if you should feel inclined to expand on the subject . . ."

"Wait for me!" said Costock. He hurried to the bar, and returned with a full tray.

Grayson took his own tankard, wished Brother Ignatius all the best, and drank deep as he looked round the room.

"Y'know," said Vere Bolding; "I don't think anyone else has ever raided the manor house since the later days of the Jacobite rising. Good Lord!"

"What did you do?" asked Longcroft. "Ring the bell, wait for him to come out, and then belt him?"

"I walked round the house until I found which room he was in," Grayson explained. "It was the gunroom. I knocked on the french window, and then stood back out of sight until he pushed it open. Then I went in."

"Press on," murmured Costock.

"As soon as Herby saw me he backed round the table and grabbed a shotgun, so I talked to him across the table, and insulted him until he became furious and careless. I edged round the table, and he reversed the gun and tried to club me with the stock. I side-stepped, rammed him in the guts with my right, and as he doubled up I swung round and clipped him on the ear with my left. Once he'd dropped the gun I gave him a chance to get his wind back, and then we mixed it. And did we mix it!"

He paused, and smiled slowly. "Herby's quite a fighter! Uses everything and nothing barred. I finally dropped him with a beauty to the heart, and left him on the deck with a sore ear'ole, a bleeding nose, and many regrets."

"And then you left the house," said Brother Ignatius.

It was a statement, and not a question, and the others glanced at him curiously.

"I left by the way I came," nodded Grayson. "Herby was waking up then, leaning on one elbow, and apparently wishing the devil to enter and fly away with me."

"You didn't see Corinne or Nat?" asked Costock.

"If they were still in the house I couldn't see Nat without seeing Corinne," Grayson replied shortly.

"Moston did not start any further trouble?" asked the little priest, meanwhile staring intently at his buckled shoes.

"I'm not sure," said Grayson. "He may have done, and he may not. It was dark, of course, apart from this scenic lightning that seems to have got out of control, and just as I was crossing Peacock I heard a noise—well, something like someone rattling the bolt on a rifle. A kind of metallic click."

"And then?"

"Two barrels were fired in some direction. I'm no gun expert, but I'd say they were shotgun noises—probably the gun Herby threatened me with. I didn't wait to investigate, but cut across to the lane and walked as far as Headley Corner and back . . ."

Hesitantly he added: "I had another of those queer bouts I had the other day. Probably the excitement. I must see a doctor when I get back to town."

"He took himself for a walk," said Brother Ignatius. "Verily the Lord protecteth His lambs."

"Thanks for that," Grayson said facetiously. "I've been a wolf in sheep's clothing for so long that it makes a nice change to be recognised as the more innocent animal!" Crewley lolled back in his seat, and looked Grayson straight in the eye. "Your affairs have so much become public property that I don't feel hesitant at asking a question. You're a southerner, aren't you?"

"Well, midlands to south."

"Wife, sister-in-law, and Moston all northerners?"

"Yes. But why do you ask?"

"We'll be gallant, and leave the two women out," said Crewley. "Never worked it out why Moston hates you?"

Grayson shrugged. "Just a natural antipathy, I suppose. If I'm to be truthful, I've always felt the same way about him. He gets under my skin."

"Nay," said Crewley, in the broadest dialect left to him after twenty years' residence in the eastern counties of England. "Trouble is you're not Sound!"

Brother Ignatius chuckled. The others merely looked as puzzled as Grayson.

"Herby has what is known up north as a Good Sitting Down. Highly respected is a Good Sitting Down!"

"With capital initial letters," the little priest reminded him.

"Aye," agreed Crewley; "with capital initials, signifying importance. Tha's forgiven owt if tha's Sound. Tha can be a liar, drunkard, fornicator, a brekker o' homes, or a ruiner o' innocent lives—so long as tha's Sound. My sister Fanny married biggest sot i' all Yorksheer, but he'd got hissen a job wi' plenty o' brass behind it, and he's sound. To be Sound is o' more importance than gaining salvation in t' chapel down t' vale."

He took a deep drink of his ale, and the room waited for him to continue.

"I've a cousin that's been assistant hangman—a proper nasty job if tha' likes. At first when he took it all t' relatives looked sideways at him. Then they found he got brass for t' job, and now he's as Sound as rest! Ee, it's a reight thing for a man to be Sound, and have a Good Sitting Down!"

Grayson signalled Costock to refill. There followed a great gulping down, in which Brother Ignatius joined.

Grayson grinned at Crewley over the froth. "Then I'm not regarded as Sound?"

"Can any man who writes be regarded as Sound by the more conventional people of the earth?" asked Crewley, his dialect slipping from him as easily as a loosened cloak.

"Yes," Costock and Longcroft said together.

"Maybe you two, yes," said Crewley, "but not a man like Grayson. Longcroft here writes only for money, so he *must* be Sound. Costock may write for money, but basically he's an amateur. He keeps a pub to make his brass—"

"And little enough does it make me," said Costock.

"Every publican in the country tells the same tale." said Crewley, dismissing the idea contemptuously. "That's hardly the point, anyway. Grayson's not like you two. He's a craftsman who earns his living by his craft, and neither a dilettante on the one hand, nor a literary prostitute on the other!"

"I don't think I like that description of myself," protested Costock.

"And I certainly don't!" said Longcroft.

"My definition of Grayson still remains valid," said Crewley. "He's a craftsman. Who was it said there was a time when soap was made to wash with, and chairs to sit on, and now both are only made to be sold? That's true of the aims of most people today."

Costock nodded. "It was James Harvey Robinson in his book, *Mind in the Making*. That's my complaint against Longcroft—he writes to sell. I couldn't do that, and on the other hand I could not take the risk of trying to earn a living by writing only what I want to write. There could be no compromise there, and so I had to compromise elsewhere. I took the pub to provide bread and butter, and still write for my own satisfaction, and the jam and honey on the b—and b—. Bran's not like that. He just couldn't compromise."

"And therefore he's not Sound," said Vere Bolding.

"Surely it is fundamentally the old story of the one white starling in the flock?" murmured Brother Ignatius. "Unless one conforms to the social conventions of the flock, or herd, or other group to which one belongs—well . . ."

"Candidly, y'know," said Vere Bolding, "I admire Grayson's attitude no end, but he's still a first-rate bloody fool!"

A quiet feminine voice from the bar corner of the room said: "It's the bloody fools of this earth that have made it a fit place to live in."

Unnoticed, Doreen Costock had slipped through the opened half-door, and stood in the shadowed corner with a glass of lemon gin in her curled fingers.

"Do go on, please," said Brother Ignatius.

"Who was a bigger fool than Marie Curie to spend her life—or a large part of it—stirring boiling cauldrons with a heavy iron rod in a rotten, damp, leaking and draughty shed? What was common opinion of her at the time? And where would the world be today without radium?"

"It's true," said Vere Bolding.

"And Flo Nightingale, and Helen Keller, and Mary Baker Eddy, and Sister Kenny, and the thousands of women—all b.f.'s—who've gone out all over the world as religious missionaries, medical missionaries, teachers, and nurses? Then look at the thousands of men fools!"

She rapped her glass down sharply on the wide shelf of the half-door. "What is a bloody fool, anyway, but someone—man or woman—who despises the line of least resistance and goes out to do something instead of spending his or her life like a cow-contented oaf? On the standards Mr. Crewley has described there can't be a bigger fool on earth than Albert Schweitzer."

She gave a bitter laugh. "I doubt if he has much of a Sitting Down!"

"All right, now," Longcroft said suddenly. "These two, Costock and Grayson—mainly your husband, Mrs. Costock—are always getting at me for my commercial outlook. I've been along the coast of North Africa, and I've seen the originals of us people, the old story-tellers, and with all their craft they're only playing on common people to get baksheesh out of them. Right! Now tell me, Mrs. Costock, what Grayson is trying to do that I ain't!"

"Not being inside his mind and heart," Doreen replied slowly, "I'm hardly in the position to speak for him, but having read nearly everything he's written I'm prepared to hazard the guess that he's trying to show the truth to people through the medium of fiction."

"Knowing it all himself?" Longcroft asked with something approaching a sneer.

Doreen shook her head. "No, it doesn't come that way, Mr. Longcroft. It comes," she said pensively, "I think it comes by opening oneself as a channel through which truth and beauty can flow from—from wherever truth and beauty come from."

"Ah! And where's *that*?" asked Longcroft.

"God," said Brother Ignatius.

Costock glanced curiously at Grayson, who was listening intently, and with some show of embarrassment. "How do you feel about it, Bran?"

"I—I don't quite know," Grayson answered uncertainly. "I don't feel that I'm a good writer, even after many years of experience, but I've always had the feeling—perhaps silly to most of you—that I'm here to do a job. It's something to do with writing, something that will come *through* writing. I've written some tripe, and I admit that, but I've always felt it was all practice and experience, a getting-ready for The Job."

"With capital initials," said Vere Bolding.

Grayson nodded. "That's correct."

Vere Bolding grimaced. "There's no wonder that Moston never understood you—nor your wife either, if you'll pardon my impertinence."

Brother Ignatius leaned forward from his corner. "If Mrs. Grayson and Moston desire Mr. Grayson to make money I suggest that they stick by him, and back him up."

"Started a fortune-telling booth now?" asked Longcroft.

"I am stating a fact," said the little priest. "It is surely summed up in the Bible, where we are told that the one who shall try to save his life shall lose it—or, as Mrs. Costock said, or implied, the one who denies himself the pleasure of taking the line of least resistance is the one who, in the end, achieves the Kingdom of Heaven! Mr. Grayson is trying to benefit his fellow-men—although he will deny that great aim—and while it may not be good material economics, Mr. Longcroft, it is certain that in the end the world will pay him more for his products than it will pay you for yours."

"That's paradoxical, but true," said Vere Bolding. "Take my plantations and woods. I could grow trees very quickly for sale, but they wouldn't be good trees with sound hearts, and my buyers would soon fade away. It's the same with other crops. I let them grow nature's way, slowly and surely, and in their own seasons. My trees, when mature, are felled, and planked, and they'll last for centuries. And what happens if you grow them for money? Blow them up with fertilisers? Make 'em grow in half the natural time? You turn 'em out with—"

He glanced over Costock's shoulder at the tall, blue-uniformed constable who had appeared from the passage.

"Costock, old man, we're in trouble. Lord, it's half an hour after time."

Costock smiled at the policeman. "All right, Burton! These gentlemen are my guests."

"Not concerned about that, sir—although you might get the other side of the house cleared. No, I wondered if you'd heard about the affair up at the manor."

Grayson suppressed a smile.

"A very nasty accident," said Burton.

"Accident?" Grayson exclaimed. "Not—not a little girl?"

The constable looked behind him to make sure that he would not be overheard, and then said in a low voice: "Big-head has half killed himself with a gun. Shot himself through the guts— pardon, ma'am, I didn't see you there. I meant through the stomach."

"Herby!" said Grayson. "It must have been an accident!"

"Why that?" asked Burton, so quickly and keenly that Costock began to eye him cautiously.

Grayson shrugged. "Just wouldn't have the nerve to shoot himself."

"Got a lot of bruises on him, too."

Grayson grinned. "He would have!"

"Now look, sir; it seems to me you know something about him. What do you mean by that remark?"

"I gave him a damned good hiding tonight," Grayson said happily. "And now he's managed to shoot himself through the stomach. Well, well! How are the mighty fallen! Tell it not in Gath; publish it not in the streets of As—"

Costock tapped him on the shoulder. "Do you mind keeping your big mouth shut, Bran. Your supper's waiting in the kitchen."

"Why should the gentleman keep his big mouth shut?" Burton demanded. "Pardon me repeating you like that, sir!"

"Burton," said Costock, "you have not told us the full truth, have you?"

"I'm a policeman, sir."

"Any other policemen in the village, Burton?"

"Well, the Inspector's up at the house with the police surgeon and another doctor."

"Then he's either not ill enough to be taken to hospital, or he's too ill!"

"He's too ill, sir," Burton said stolidly. "If you must know the truth, they're going to operate on him on the gunroom table straight away. They're just waiting for gas and stuff to be brought from Yeagrave Cottage Hospital. He's blown off some of his lung, and severely damaged his liver."

"You look tired, Burton," Costock said solicitously. "Think you could risk a drink?"

"On duty, sir?"

"On duty, Burton, and a free packet of chlorophyl tablets thrown in. Hang it, man, they can't expect you to keep going on fresh air!"

"Well, put that way, sir . . ."

It was put that way, and it was put down, several times, and Burton mellowed considerably in the next twenty minutes.

Longcroft slipped away without being noticed. Crewley said his goodnights openly. Harry Vere Bolding slapped his tweed hat on his head, took his ash stick from its usual corner by the hearth, and announced that if bearers should be needed he would be only too pleased to oblige.

Brother Ignatius left with Crewley, saying there was a possibility he might prove of use up at the manor house.

Burton was meanwhile lured step by step to the kitchen, where Doreen had hurriedly prepared a plate piled high with ham sandwiches.

"Help yourself," Costock said casually. "You, Bran?"

Grayson took the hint to be matey, held the plate to Burton, and took a sandwich himself.

"How on earth did Moston do it?" Costock asked between munches.

"Nobody seems to know, sir," said Burton. "His wife went looking for him, and found him just inside the door of the gun-room, near dying. He was sprawled on his face and the gun was under him."

"Certainly sounds like an accident," said Costock, with a wise nod of his head. "He was a townee, and knew nothing of guns. Probably carrying it with the spout upwards, and tripped, and—well, you've lived in country districts longer than I have, Burton. Another sandwich?"

"I'm afraid I must be going. The Boss told me not to be too long!"

"Doing what?" Costock asked as innocently as he could.

"Why, making inquiries, sir!"

"Of course—but about what?"

Burton looked surprised at Costock's ignorance. "Why, *you* know, sir! Who had been up to the manor, and when, and had they seen anything or anybody suspicious? You know!"

"I was getting a bit dim," said Costock. "The time of night and all that. It's getting on for half-past eleven."

Doreen extended her hand towards the constable. "The tablets, Mr. Burton. Mustn't have your breath smelling! They might make you walk white lines and recite the little poem about the Leith polithe dithmithing uth."

Burton grinned, and thanked her, and Costock steered him towards the front door and got rid of him. He returned to the kitchen, scowling heavily at Grayson.

"You get better! No more wits than a child of five! What made you open your big trap like that? Telling him you'd bashed up Herby!"

"Well, it sounded like an accident," Grayson said somewhat sheepishly.

"It probably was, but how's it going to sound if Herby kicks the bucket? What if there's an inquest, and your story has to come out? Ever met old Kinglade?"

"Who's Kinglade?"

"The District Coroner. He can make four out of two plus two better than anybody I know. I can just imagine the sensation in court. You admit wiping up Herby in gladiatorial style, and he's found with a belly full of shot!"

Costock covered his eyes with a hand. "Oh glory! I can see it now. Old Kinglade sitting there asking you questions about your own statement, and Inspector Wing standing at the back of the court waiting for a verdict that will entitle him to clap his hand on your shoulder as you try to leave. Bah . . . !"

"Herby'll probably get better—I'm afraid," said Grayson.

"I ain't much of a hand at prayer," said Costock, "but I'm praying for Herby—for your sake—this night and every night until he's walking upright again."

"Adam Zad, the bear that walks like a man," quoted Grayson. "Er—considering the serious view you seem to be taking, do you think I should stick around here tomorrow?"

Costock winced. "Let's have it? What had you in mind?"

"Slipping out quietly about four in the morning, and walking back to town, or part way back, and then bussing it. I'd like to see the dawn. It's some time since I did, and it's really the only time a man can be alone with his own soul."

"He's also alone with it in the dock at Norwich Assizes," Costock said dryly. "It's quite possible for Herby to die of wounds, you know!"

"Not Herby!"

"Apart from which," Costock went on, as if he had not been interrupted, "you've had a pretty gruelling week-end, just in case you hadn't noticed it. You need a good rest."

Grayson smiled whimsically. "Okay! Little Bran will do as he's told, and go to bed to sleep the sleep of the just."

"The simple-minded always do sleep well," Costock said. "Having little or no mind they can have little on it. And don't forget to pray for Herby!"

Grayson paused in the doorway. "I try to live a righteous life, even if the fact isn't recognised by my relatives and some of my erstwhile friends, but there are some things beyond all expectation of fulfilment. Night-night both of you—and thanks for everything!"

"Don't mention it—much," grinned Costock. "Many duties and obligations are laid on the shoulders of an innkeeper, but the blue book never mentioned you."

Grayson went to his room, and without switching on the light flung the casement wide and leaned on the sill, to look wonderingly towards the manor house. The electric storm was dying away, and only occasional flashes of lightning tore the velvet purple of the night sky, but the manor was alive with light. There appeared to be a deal of activity. Car lights came and went, and a strong beam which could conceivably have been a floodlight streamed from the centre of the Peacock Lawn in the direction of the gun-room doors.

Grayson grimaced. Herby was apparently causing a deal of trouble to somebody. It seemed incredible that such a thing should have happened so soon after he left. How on earth had Herby been so careless as to shoot himself through the stomach? Still, the morning would probably provide the answer. In the meantime, it was near midnight, and he was beginning to realise that he was nearly all in. He got undressed, and got into bed.

V
Emissary of Justice

GRAYSON AWOKE at four in the morning. He lay for some time, staring into the darkness, and let the incidents of the previous hours project themselves on the silver screen of his mind, and when there was no more film left he began to reflect upon their possible consequences. With Herby wounded so efficiently that an emergency operation had been necessary he would be in bed for some weeks, and so out of harm's way—or out of the way of doing any further harm. Which meant that Natalie was safe. And in any case she was either at Yarmouth, or her mother would be taking her during the morning, and even a fit Herby was not likely to pursue her there.

Then there was Corinne. She was only too obviously the victim of the emotional strain of the past few weeks, and the best thing was to leave her severely alone, in the hope that she would come back to him of her own volition. He most certainly did not intend to entice her back by either threat or promise. Throughout their married life he had respected her in accordance with his belief that wives were not chattels, but individuals, and if on occasion he had been tempted to order her comings and goings, and decisions, he had always restrained himself, and made his feelings—perhaps they were instincts—obey the dictates of his reason. He had, on occasion, wondered if he was wise, and if his belief was not founded on idealism rather than on the experience of husbands throughout the ages. Be that as it may, he intended to follow the path he had chosen. It was going to be hard for some time; to avoid seeing Corinne meant sacrificing the companionship of Natalie, for it would be impossible to visit the child either at Wingford or Yarmouth without meeting her mother.

He blinked into the darkness. In that case there was no further reason for him to stay in the village. He could get back to town straight away and press on with the all-important novel.

He swung out of bed, and dressed. He fumbled together his few belongings and crammed them into the rucksack, and then tiptoed down the stairs with his rucksack, burberry, and shoes. He found his way to the kitchen, where he switched on the light long enough to put on his shoes, and raid Doreen's pantry for the remainder of the sandwiches left by Burton. Then he threaded his arms through the rucksack straps, let himself from the house, and strode blithely down the road.

It grew bitterly cold in the half-hour of the false dawn, and he quickened his step. He watched the dawn, and experienced its mysterious stillness, from the top of a five-barred gate between Wymondham and Thetford.

He returned to his room in Norfolk Square at nine o'clock.

He had been in the house little more than twenty minutes when his bell rang, and going to the door he found a dark-coated, and bowler-hatted man on the step, a man with thick black brows, and the thickest, wildest, and blackest walrus-type moustache Grayson had ever seen on any man.

"Mr. Grayson, by any chance? Mr. Brandreth Grayson?"

"That's me," said Grayson.

"I wonder . . . Could I come inside for a minute. It's parky here on the step, and—er—not too private."

Grayson nodded. "Come in by all means. I'm making a cup of coffee if you'd care to join me."

The moustache followed him to the room.

Grayson closed the door, and his visitor produced a ready-charged and much-stained meerschaum pipe from his pocket and stuck it between his teeth.

"Why have you come to see *me*, Sergeant?"

"We-ell," Ellis replied lightly, as if the matter was one of no real importance. "We-ell, there are one or two things we don't know about your brother-in-law which we think you might be able to tell us."

Grayson nodded. "How true that is! But look—and perhaps I'm obtuse—but why are Scotland Yard making the inquiries?"

"Main reason is that the county police asked us to help, of course."

"I see . . ." said Grayson.

He made two cups of coffee with the milk and a bottle of essence. He handed one to Ellis. "Sugar on the sideboard. Deadly stuff this bottled tack, to a decent palate, but I haven't the time to play about with the percolator." He stared at Ellis, and tried to widen the slits of his weary eyes. "It doesn't sound like an accident. The whole thing's darned ridiculous, actually, because Herby hadn't the guts to shoot himself. Why should he, anyway?"

"Why should he?" Ellis echoed in the blandest of tones. "That's apparently what the C.C. thought about it."

"The C.C.?"

"Chief Constable."

"Oh yes, of course."

Grayson waved a hand. "I forgot to ask you to sit down, Sergeant. There's a chair behind you."

Ellis did not accept the invitation. He took the hot coffee down at one swallow, pushed the pipe back in his mouth, and said: "You were down at Wingford during the week-end, weren't you?"

"I was in the village when it happened. I must have been, judging by what Burton told us."

"Burton? Do I know him?"

"Village bobby. He came making inquiries about half-ten last night."

"Where was this?" asked Ellis.

"In the pub, the Barley Mow. I was staying there with the landlord and his wife, Mr. and Mrs. Costock. They are personal friends."

Ellis shuffled, and appeared to be disturbed about something.

"You'll forgive me asking this, Mr. Grayson, but were you at the manor house last night?"

"I certainly was, Sergeant."

"You saw your brother-in-law?"

"I certainly did."

"Did he see you?"

"Most certainly."

Ellis smiled. "Three certainties on each side adds up to six. Up to now I've only known of three—rent day, death, and the wife expecting. However . . . ! Was he alive when you left him, Mr. Grayson?"

Grayson closed one eye and regarded the sergeant cautiously with the other. He was now seeing signs of danger, and began to retreat to a position not previously prepared. "He was alive," he said shortly.

"May I put it to you quite bluntly that you and he had a row—and a fight, Mr. Grayson."

"If Burton is as good a constable as I suspect, then you know exactly what I said in his presence last night, Mr. Ellis. The row took place some considerable time before the fight—and the village should have told you all about that!"

"You agree that you talked about the scrap in the pub?"

"I've just told you so. I gave a round by round summary."

"What shape was he in when you left?"

"Pretty poor, I hope!"

Ellis said: "We're trying to help the doc by separating the damage you did to him from the damage he collected afterwards."

"I hit him in the solar plexus, and then punched his chin. The next few minutes were in the nature of a scrimmage, but in the main I went for his head."

"Why that?"

"He was a thick man, and his head was the thickest bit of the lot, so I reckoned that if I beat his head I had well and truly beaten the whole man."

"That," said Ellis, producing a notebook and pen, "must be noted down for posterity. It's just about the most original remark I've ever heard about a fight. Who won?"

"Me," said Grayson. "I repeated the first two blows, and laid him low on the gun-room floor."

"You never gravitated outside the room, Mr. Grayson?"

"It was a spot waltz, not a Paul Jones," Grayson said solemnly.

"Excuse me," Ellis said with a grin. "That also must be registered in my joke book."

"While he was taking the count," continued Grayson, "I bade him a soldier's farewell, and left the house."

"How?" Ellis asked laconically.

"By going back over the same route. I lit a cigarette before leaving, and you'll probably find the match stick on the floor. I flipped it at him as a gesture of contempt. Herby was then coming round, and slowly pulling himself into a sitting position."

"I see," said Ellis. "Then what did you do?"

"Went for a walk."

"You heard shots—or so I'm told."

"Two barrels of a shot gun."

"Think they were fired at you?"

"I wouldn't know," said Grayson. "I heard a click, not unlike the bolt of a rifle being shot home, and changed direction in the interests of private security—making for the cover of the yew hedges."

"You didn't hear any phewing over your head—like shot whistling over?"

"No, but then the shots came some time after the clicking. As a matter of fact, now I come to think about it, I must have been clear of the grounds by then."

Ellis put away notebook and pen. "Thanks for all that, sir. Decent of you to be so co-operative. It helps us to separate the two incidents. By the way, you'll be willing to state all you've told me in writing, and sign it?"

"Oh yes, Sergeant. Why not?"

"That's a point," said Ellis. "I'll be able to find you here—say tomorrow—if necessary?"

"Either here, or back at Wingford, or up at Yarmouth if my wife should want me. Truth to tell, I'm not quite sure where she is at the moment."

"I see," said Ellis. "I've heard something of your background, of course. Rumour travels faster than straight truth. You didn't get on very well with Moston, did you?"

"We didn't get on well with each other. Hated each other's guts."

"Any particular reason?" Ellis asked in a casual tone that suggested that he could not have cared less.

Grayson gave a wry smile. "Crewley suggested that it was because Herby had a Good Sitting Down. Herby was Sound, and I wasn't."

"That's as clear as a fortune-teller's crystal in a coal cellar," said Ellis.

"You're going to Wingford again?" asked Grayson. As Ellis nodded he said: "You'll meet Crewley down there, if you haven't already met him. He's the estate bailiff for Moston, and can probably explain more fully and capably than I can."

Ellis nodded his head up and down as if trying to shake an idea into it. "Herby had a Good Sitting Down, and you were not Sound—judging by the intonation and inflexion and a few other grammatical terms those phrases, in print, would be in italics?"

"Or with capital initials," said Grayson. He was beginning to enjoy himself now that danger seemed to have passed. "I believe they are purely north-country terms."

"When did you leave Wingford, Mr. Grayson?"

Grayson suppressed a smile. "About half past four this morning."

"Why? It's a rum time to leave your bed, isn't it?"

"I wanted to see the dawn."

Ellis blinked, and put his pipe in his pocket. "You what . . . ?"

"Wanted to see the dawn!"

"What the hell for?"

"Have you never seen the dawn?" Grayson asked guilelessly.

"Plenty of times, but I wouldn't get up to see it. Wouldn't get up deliberately, that is. What's it got that a sunset hasn't?"

"A sunset's when the sun's going down."

"Well, yes! I learned that at school," said Ellis.

"Dawn's when it is coming up."

Ellis looked him over, and hastened to agree. "Yes, I see it now, Mr. Grayson. All the difference in the world, isn't there? Yes, of course. Silly of me!"

Then he paused, and did a double-take on the matter. "Look, Mr. Grayson," he said; "either you're magnoon—which is Arabic for bats or loopy, or I'm as dim as Toc H Lamp. What *is* the difference?"

Grayson stared through Ellis, and through the wall, and across London to the open country. He turned time upside down, and chased it down the spiral of the hours to its daily beginning.

"Darkness follows the sunset, but light follows the dawn. In that short time before sunrise the early world awakes again and there come dim stirrings of the primeval past. Forgotten racial memories rise from the ancient mind to the threshold of consciousness. At that time Man is closer to God than at any other—closer to his unknown self, the immortal self that has accompanied him throughout eternity in the myriad recurrences of his existence. There comes an irresistible uprush of wisdom and understanding from the bosom of the earth, and with the first rays of the sun the supreme creative power of the universe flows down to give life to man for yet another day . . ."

He broke off, and asked: "Ever read *The Wind in the Willows*, Sergeant? Remember the piper at the gates of dawn?"

"I go for westerns, myself," said Ellis.

Grayson continued to stare through the materialistic and bewildered Ellis.

"At sunset there is a gradual withdrawing of all power, a protective concentration. All things are tight-folded and concealing—so what is the use of a sunset to any artist, whether he uses paint, or words, or stone?"

"You tell me," said Ellis.

He shook himself, and hugged his coat to him as if he had suddenly gone cold. "Well, thanks for everything, Mr. Grayson. We've learned a lot about each other in a short time, haven't we?"

"That's a questionable statement, Sergeant," said Grayson.

He accompanied Ellis to the door and saw him off the premises. When he was gone he unlocked his desk and sat down to write up his journal. Facts, feelings, and thoughts went down without stint, and when he finally closed the book he felt both cleansed and refreshed. He slipped off his shoes, lay on the bed, and pulled the eiderdown over himself.

He slept until one o'clock, and then got up, washed, had a snack, and got down to the typewriter to work on the novel. But for two hourly pauses for drinks he worked through the day, and the evening, and finally got undressed and into bed at half past one the next morning.

He awoke at ten o'clock, and pulled on his dressing-gown to go through to the hall to collect his mail and the daily paper. Still bleary-eyed, he sat in the window seat to sort his mail, and found a telegram. It was from Michael Costock, and characteristically terse: *"If you feel like a walk, walk this way. You are wanted. Mike."*

He put it aside without bothering to consider what it might imply. The letters were of no importance, and he turned to the morning paper. The middle column of the front page carried a solid black heading: YARD CALLED TO EAST ANGLIA MURDER.

He blinked at it. It was odd, very odd that there should be a murder down there at the same time as Herby's puzzling death.

And then he read the first line, and went on to complete the first paragraph, and so down to the black rule that marked the end of the story.

He filled the kettle and put it on the gas ring, and went back to the paper. It was some seconds later that he jumped so quickly that he bumped his head on the window.

"Good God, no! Herby—murdered!"

He re-read the story, and a cold cord began to wind itself round his heart. Mrs. Corinne Grayson, wife of novelist Brandreth Grayson, had twice been interviewed yesterday by Superintendent Gordon Knollis, of New Scotland Yard. It was understood that she had made a statement "of considerable help to the police" after visiting Yeagrave Police Station with the Superintendent, and Inspector Wing, of the County C.I.D. . . . .

Professor A. B. C. Dorking, Britain's foremost pathologist, known affectionately in police and newspaper circles as Mr. Alphabet, had travelled through the previous night from his home to conduct a long post-mortem examination . . .

Finger-print and other experts arrived at Wingford at intervals throughout the day, but no statement was yet available from the police . . .

A brief addenda had been fudged into the stop press column: "Professor Dorking completed his autopsy on Moston shortly before noon yesterday it is understood, and his report is expected by the police early today."

Grayson tipped back his head, and stared at the ceiling. Herby was certainly not liked, but who on earth, apart from himself, hated him sufficiently to even think of murder?

And suddenly he knew the answer. He knew why Ellis had called on him, and what Mike Costock's telegram meant.

He dressed hurriedly, sorted all the coppers and sixpences from his loose change, and hurried out to the call box at the corner of the street. There was a telephone in the house, but he did not want his Cockney concierge to hear what he had to say—and she usually missed nothing.

He dialled New Scotland Yard, and asked for Sergeant George Ellis. Ellis, he was informed, was out. Could anyone else help, or would he care to leave a message.

He said neither, and hurried back to the house. A long black saloon car stood outside the door, and a heavy black moustache hung through the near-side front window.

"Busy, Mr. Grayson?"

"Sergeant Ellis!" said Grayson. "I've just tried to phone you at the Yard. I've only just seen a paper—I worked all day and half the night. I wanted you to know I'm going back to Wingford on the first bus from Aldgate—"

Ellis beamed at him. "Now there's a coincidence! This constable is about to drive *me* to Wingford. Could we offer you a lift?"

"You wouldn't mind?"

"No inconvenience at all," Ellis assured him. "Collect the luggage and bird cage and kitchen stove, and climb in the back."

Grayson hurried indoors, still only half awake and repacked his rucksack, encased his typewriter, pushed a half ream of paper, a quire of carbon paper, and the finished pages of the novel in a despatch case, and carried the load out to Ellis's car, where the sergeant was confiding *sotto voce* to his driver that this cove was either the most innocent bloke on earth, or the one most anxious to set himself into quod that he had ever met.

"Decent of you," said Grayson as he piled himself and his belongings into the back of the car.

"All part of the Moston need service," Ellis assured him. "Trouble and distance no object. We aim to please you."

From time to time during the journey Ellis regarded Grayson covertly through the driving mirror, whose angle, to the driver's private annoyance, he altered to suit himself.

They were passing through Colchester when he made up his mind about Grayson, and whispered to his companion: "This chap's not a murderer, and he's not bats. The poor devil's suffering from shock—bad shock, too. I wonder what hell he's been through lately? I'll have to tip off the Guv'nor to treat him gently, or we'll really have a mental case on our hands."

A mile outside Yeagrave he said: "Drop me off at the station, and take Mr. Grayson on to the pub at Wingford. He has friends there who'll look after him. I'll give them a ring, meanwhile. We need him looked after. He may have the solution to the whole thing behind that clouded brain."

VI
Parley of Suspects

MICHAEL COSTOCK greeted Grayson casually as he manoeu-vred himself and his luggage through the kitchen doorway late in the afternoon.

"Have a nice walk the other morning, Bran?"

Grayson nodded. "Got a bit nippy round about dawn, but otherwise it was quite pleasant."

"How did you get here today?"

"Oh, the sergeant from the Yard happened to be outside the house, and gave me a lift here. Decent bloke! I didn't think the Yard went in for giving lifts like that."

Costock leaned on the doorway and considered him as if he was a rare animal in a zoo. Then, as the bell shrilled, he went to the telephone, and mainly listened for the next three min-utes. He considered Grayson still more thoughtfully when he re-turned, and sat across a chair with his arms folded on the back as Doreen gave Grayson a cup of tea.

"You'd better not talk in your sleep tonight. That well-known and much-publicised sleuth, Gordon Knollis, will be sleeping in the next room to yours tonight. Your charitable lift-giver, Ellis, is in the third guest room. Both will probably spend the night with their ear 'oles pressed hard against the wall paper."

"Why?" asked Grayson.

"In case you confess to shooting Herby."

"But I didn't shoot Herby!" Grayson protested.

"Quite," said Costock. "You know you didn't shoot Herby. I know you didn't shoot Herby. Doreen knows you didn't shoot Herby. It could be that the Yard men even hope that you didn't shoot Herby—but they have to prove it, and then find out who did!"

He looked hard at Grayson. "You didn't shoot Herby, did you?"

Grayson ran his tongue round the inside of his cheek and looked all round the kitchen before he answered: "I don't think so, Mike. Truth to tell, I can't remember a thing after hearing that clicking noise until just before I walked in here. I know I got to Headley Corner, and I'm pretty sure someone bade me goodnight as I left the grounds and stepped to the road, but who it was, or what happened I don't know. My head went a bit queer the night Herby and Corinne both slung me off, but I didn't want to mention it in case you and Doreen should start worrying about me."

"Now there's a thing!" said Costock, with a significant glance at his wife. "We should never have known if he hadn't told us, should we?"

"What am I supposed to do about it?" asked Grayson.

"Keep your big mouth closed is one good piece of advice. I ask you—what do you do as soon as Burton walks in? Start telling him that you had been to the house; that you had beaten up Herby, and left him on the gun-room floor in a parlous condition. Right, say the police. This is an old trick! It's the next best trick to providing a perfectly faked alibi. Admit socking the man—but as for doing anything else to him, oh no, Sir!"

"Well," Grayson said stubbornly. "I did sock him, and I didn't do anything else to him."

Costock walked round the kitchen with a well-simulated appearance of utter weariness. "Wash and brush up, and then come down for a meal. Go on! Clear out! My patience is so nearly exhausted that any minute now I'll get down on all fours and chew the carpet."

Grayson ambled easily to the doorway, and there paused. "Er—heard anything about Nat and Corinne?"

Costock exchanged glances with his wife as Grayson mentioned his child before his wife.

"They went to Yarmouth this afternoon, quite early—after the police had pumped them both dry."

"Both? You mean they . . . ?"

"They did," Costock said bluntly. "What they thought they were likely to get from Natalie, I don't profess to know, but either Knollis or Wing had a talk with her."

"They'll be safe enough with Aunt Florrie," said Grayson. "And Gwen? How has she taken it?"

"The last I heard was from Alice Day, who is quite a reliable authority on anything that happens up at the 'all," answered Costock. "Your sister-in-law was last seen galumphing through the picture gallery with a notebook and pencil, totting up how much the art treasures were worth in libri, solidi, and denari, or common coin of the realm. She had already done the furniture, and rumour hath it that she'll sell Wingford, and hit it back to the bright lights of London or Leeds."

"That's one better than the prince," said Grayson. Costock raised an inquiring eyebrow. "Prince?"

"The one who tried on the crown before the old man had cocked his toes heavenwards."

"She's obviously a woman of deep sensibilities," said Costock. "Now push off, friend, and get the smell of the Big Smoke cleansed from your flesh."

Grayson took his luggage to his room, and stripped to the waist to go to the bathroom. It may or may not have been coincidence, but on the landing he collided with a sleek, grey-clad man. He said: "Sorry!"

The other also apologised, and then looked a second time. "Mr. Grayson by any chance?"

"I admit it."

"I'm Gordon Knollis—New Scotland Yard, you know!" Grayson grimaced; almost winced. He had heard a great deal about Knollis during the past few years, but this was his first sight of the man. Physically, he was of medium height, a naturally slimmish man filling out, as he aged, at the dictates of his glands. His cheek bones were high. His jaw was firm without being in the rat-trap classification. His nose was long and straight, but not narrow. Indulging in somewhat amateurish character-reading, Grayson decided he was a man with a one-track mind and a great deal of pertinacity behind it. If anyone could resolve the mystery of Herby's death, Knollis was probably the man.

"I've heard of you," said Grayson.

"I'll have to have a word with you at some more suitable time, Mr. Grayson."

Grayson nodded. "In about five or ten minutes I'll be taking tea in the sitting-room. Perhaps you'd care to join me?"

"Thank you. I'll do that." Knollis said.

Grayson took his time over his wash. There were things to be thought about, and his mind was still working slowly, and not too well.

Knollis obviously went straight down and spoke to Costock, for when Grayson eventually ambled into the kitchen Costock jerked his thumb in the direction of the sitting-room.

"The dick's in there—waiting. Doreen can't provide mint tea, nor yet the fragrant sweepings of the floor of the Beautiful House of Rozzers of the Yangtse Valley, but don't forget the mandarin rules—it gives one time to prepare one's story. One sips, and talks about the weather, and the state of the rice crops, and the relative merits of the geishas—or am I wandering into Japan? Anyway, each sums up the other, and not until the tea cups are laid aside does one mention business. I could, if pressed, supply the detective gentleman with treacle toffee sandwiches in order to delay the meal."

He waved an airy hand. "Still, I expect he knows the rules. The man has a manner, a courtesy, generally not found in dicks. Er—Bran . . . ?" he asked more seriously.

"Mm?"

"Feeling better? More normal and all that?"

Grayson ran a hand over the crown of his head. "Funny you should ask that. It's sort of numb all across here, as if the blood supply isn't getting to my brain. Why do you ask?"

Costock demurred. "We-ell, you've had what can be described as quite a couple of days, haven't you?"

"Quite a couple of days—or is it three? Damned if I know what day it is. Time and the days don't seem to mean anything any more. Oh well, I'd better go and get this do over, and then I can perhaps try to concentrate my mind on what I'm going to do about Nat and Corinne."

He went quickly to the sitting-room, and did not hear Costock say: "Like a lamb to the slaughter, poor devil! Something has to be done!"

Knollis was standing in the bow window, his hands in his trouser pockets. Afternoon tea was already laid out on the coffee table, and two cups of tea were poured.

Knollis was quite affable, even if slightly cynical as he nodded to the table and remarked that he was sorry if it looked a little too much like the spread laid out by the spider to entice the fly.

Grayson flicked the suggestion aside with thumb and fore-finger. "Mandarin rules, Mr. Knollis. I believe in gracious living, so shall we eat and drink, and talk of shoes, and ships, and sealing wax, and cabbages and kings?"

Knollis fell in with his mood. As they seated themselves he added: "And why the sea is boiling hot, and whether pigs have wings?"

"Bread and butter, Mr. Knollis?"

"Thank you. The jam?"

"Thank *you*."

A slight, cassocked figure passed the window, and turned in at the adjoining door.

"You know Brother Ignatius by any chance?" asked Knollis.

"I travelled down with him on the morning train," said Grayson. "Most cultured little man. You know him?"

"One of my very few friends, Mr. Grayson. From time to time we meet in a little place in Bridge Street—"

"Opposite the Houses of Parliament."

"You know it?"

"I do," said Grayson. "But you were saying . . . ?"

"Oh yes! We meet there, and discuss mutual problems." Knollis gave a short laugh. "I should say we talk about worldly matters known to me, and more unworldly ones which are commonplace matters to Ignatius, and mysteries to me."

Grayson's lips twitched with concealed amusement.

"Ouspensky, and Lahsen, and time-spirals, and six-dimensional continuums, and eternal recurrence, and such matters?"

Knollis raised an eyelid. "How do you know?"

"After several hours natter with your diminutive friend I flatter myself as a continually observing author that I correctly estimated the man's intellectual level. May I pour you more tea?"

"Please," said Knollis. "Such subjects are commonplace to you also?"

"Put it this way," said Grayson as he handed back Knollis's filled cup. "The subject is an oft-discussed one, but I continually pray with Solomon for wisdom and understanding."

"You understand much of these strange teachings?"

Grayson poured himself a second cup before answering. "Gurdjieff said little outside the circle of his chosen disciples. Ouspensky said quite a lot, and more openly. Rudolf Steiner wrote so much that it is difficult to correlate his various teachings. Lahsen, on the other hand, threw out his teachings in the language of the common man, and reduced to the simplest possible terms, working on the principle that those with ears to hear would hear, and those who had not would not—that way he avoided the injunction against casting pearls before swine, and casting that which is holy to the dogs. Lahsen believed that we were all gods in the making . . ."

As an afterthought he added: "There were others, you know! The search for absolute truth is going on all over the world."

"It is time that fascinates me," murmured Knollis. "Ignatius has tried to make me understand, but I just can't—can't—"

"Visualise time as an eternal now?" asked Grayson. Then, seeing that Knollis was at the end of his meal he turned the conversation to Herby Moston's death, determined to get it over.

"Time, of course, will interest you. It is such a vital factor in your work, isn't it?"

Knollis smiled at him. "All right, Mr. Grayson! What would you like to tell me?"

"What do you want to know?"

"All you care to tell me. I have plenty of—time."

"This house is several centuries old, Mr. Knollis," Grayson mused. "Wouldn't it be odd if we had gone through all this before? You as a Bow Street Runner, and myself as an itinerant chapman or ballad-monger? However, do you wish me to go right back to the days when I was trying to court my wife, and brother-in-law Herby was trying to keep me away from her? Or just from when I came here—Good God," he exclaimed, "was it only as recently as Saturday?"

"From Saturday," said Knollis. "The rest of the story will emerge."

An hour later Knollis spoke for the first time, and Grayson sagged in his chair and tried to clear the creeping cobwebs from his brain.

"You have been very frank, Mr. Grayson. I should be equally frank with you. No fingerprints of yours were found on the gun. We also ascertained that you were not wearing gloves on that day—who would, in late summer?"

"Then why the devil let me reel all that lot off my mind?" Grayson demanded angrily. "Dammit, I've gone back over eleven or twelve years!"

"Yes, but in doing so you've told me a lot about Moston."

Grayson bent over the table. "I never was under suspicion of killing Herby!"

"Whoever said you were?" asked Knollis with the blandest of smiles. "Tell me, Mr. Grayson; were you ever envious or covetous of Moston's—er—Good Sitting Down?"

Grayson found himself unable to suppress a grin. "You've been talking to Crewley!"

"Quite an interesting chat!" said Knollis. "Unfortunately, Mr. Grewley's hypothesis only complicates the case because—it would seem—so many people actively disliked Moston without actually hating him."

Grayson glanced at the wall clock. "They're open now. Care to adjourn to the smoke-room for a drink? No one else will be in for an hour."

Knollis considered the suggestion, and then nodded. "All right, Mr. Grayson."

Before the smoke-room fireplace, with glasses of bitter before them, Grayson answered the question Knollis had asked some minutes before.

"I didn't envy Herby. I'd like a place similar to Wingford—and who wouldn't—but I'd like to earn it with the ability of my brain and the agility of my fingers across a set of typewriter keys. There was no covetousness. Crewley's Good Sitting Down, just for the sake of it, doesn't appeal to me at all. Funny, that . . ." he said, staring into space.

"What is?" asked Knollis.

"After Herby had kicked me from his threshold I had a few minutes with my kiddy. I talked Grown Up to her, trying to instil into her the difference between liking things for how much they cost, and appreciating them for their true worth. And now you raise the same question. No, Mr. Knollis! If I'd been interested in a Good Sitting Down for its social and monetary values I should have pulled out and let Dickinson go to the bottom of the sea alone, but he was trying to do something worth while. We both were. Trouble was that I . . ."

"Yes, Mr. Grayson?"

"Skip it," said Grayson. "Herby believed that when you were dead you were done for, and consequently had to make the best of this life because you never got another!"

"And you?"

Grayson raised his eyes and looked straightly at Knollis. "Some of us know better."

"You, and Brother Ignatius—and Lahsen!"

"And others," said Grayson softly.

They were disturbed by the arrival of Harry Vere Bolding. He put his ash stick in the corner, hung his tweed hat on the antlers over the door, and waited until Costock, after a quick glance round the angle of the door brought his tankard. Then he nodded, and said: "Good evening."

"We were just discussing Herby's philosophy," said Grayson, with a wink of the eye furthest away from Knollis.

"Didn't know he had one," said Vere Bolding. He took down half the contents of the tankard, and then lit his pipe. Then he said: "The night before last I offered to be a bearer at his funeral. Or was it last night? Time seems to have spun itself into a web during the past few days. Anyway, that offer stands."

"You didn't like him?" said Knollis.

Grayson hastened to introduce them.

"I know you by repute, sir," said Vere Bolding. "Glad to know you, but not on this visit. You should go away and let the village benefactor spend the rest of his life in peace, and with the good wishes of the villagers to lighten the burden of his days. After all, to kill even a man like Moston must be disturbing to the soul at times."

"Like that, eh?"

Grayson signalled to Costock, and the conversation lapsed until the return of the tray.

"On the house," said Costock. "Here's health, and luck to some!"

Knollis wryly acknowledged the left-handed toast. "I doubt if I've ever been so aware of my unpopularity."

Vere Bolding snorted. "The fault doesn't lie with you, sir. You represent the law, which must be observed, but the law should learn to close its eyes at times."

"How did Moston offend the village?" asked Knollis.

"He came, sir, loaded with cash and empty of culture. He attempted to wipe his uneducated and presumably unwashed feet on the sweet green grass of a decent English village that was here before Agincourt."

Costock added: "Putting Herby down in Wingford was like Gainsborough giving Gloriana, Duchess of Devonshire, a turnip to hold while she posed for him."

"He should never have come!" fumed Vere Bolding.

"All things are lawful, but not all things are expedient," said a quiet voice. Brother Ignatius joined them, and Costock went to the bar and returned with a froth-topped pint of bitter beer.

"You also knew him, Ignatius?" said Knollis.

"I had business with him," said the little priest. "That is why I came to Wingford on Saturday. I suppose I should tell you this? He was going to turn old Mrs. Walters from her cottage, and knock it down. He *said* it spoiled the view from his library windows . . ."

"It's a good quarter of a mile away!" exploded Costock. "There must have been some other reason."

"And he'd sacked me if anybody's interested," said Crewley as he entered the room. "Ruddy 'opeless I was. Couldn't make him more than eight per cent profit on the ruddy estate. General idea seemed to be that you can't have a Good Sitting Down on less than ten per cent."

"This—er—Good Sitting Down seems to have been an important factor in the cause of Moston's death," Knollis said quietly. "These varying standards and values could almost have been the root cause."

"Wouldn't be surprised at all," said Crewley.

He glanced down the passage as footsteps sounded on the stone flags. "Here's the only man in the village Moston respected. Our village tripe-writer, Mr. Paul Longcroft."

"Evening one and all, and a little less of that, Mr. Crewley, please," said Longcroft. He looked round for Costock. "Usual—Mister—Sir—Cock, please."

He nodded affably to Knollis. "You're the rozzer from the Yard, I take it? Pleased to meet you, sir—"

"Thanks," said Knollis dryly.

"And luck with your quest—bad luck!"

"Thanks again. This time for nothing," said Knollis. "Suppose I buy this round, Mr. Costock. It would seem I have to pay my way into the village."

"We'll accept your beer." said Longcroft, "because we've no pride in that respect. For the rest, you've had it, chum! I'm a foreigner. Grayson's a foreigner. Crewley's a foreigner, and he's been here almost since Noah made a three-point landing on Ararat. I'm not sure about the colonel," he said, looking dubiously at Vere Bolding. "Perhaps in his case it's the village that's a foreigner, because they do say his family was here before the village."

"Actually, they were," said Vere Bolding. "The village grew up around the manor and the church. The manor house was first, of course, and later the church was built by my ancestors to the glory of a beneficent God, and so that therein might worship the family and their retainers."

"Then the village hasn't been here since before Agincourt?" said Knollis.

"Oh God, sir, no! Give me a little dramatic licence!

"The manor was built between the years 1615 and 1620. The church was begun some fifteen years later. The family really is in Domesday Book, but it was scattered round the county until old Francis Vere Bolding built the house and drew its members under one roof. Don't take that too literally either, sir! What he actually did was build several houses in the neighbourhood, and bring the family into the immediate area of Wingford."

"It must have hurt you to see it go?" Knollis suggested.

"Ye-es, it did, but it hurt my brother far more. He was probably the last of the Tories to realise that the old order changeth, giving place to the new. As the elder brother, Wingford was his responsibility and obligation. When the penny eventually dropped, it dropped thoroughly, and he knew Wingford had gone from the Vere Boldings for ever. That's true even though Moston is dead."

"Your brother? Where is he now?"

"He cleared off to South America—to Chile. He sank what money he had left in nitrate mining. The poor devil wanted to get clear away, being sick at heart—especially as he had the misfortune to meet Moston on one occasion, at the lawyer's."

"He has not returned to England?" asked Knollis.

"No, he did not come back to murder Moston," said Vere Bolding.

Knollis gave him a penetrating glance, and left. Longcroft looked hard at the glowing end of his cigarette. "I think I'm beginning to get the hang of it," he said. "I mean all this culture and tradition stuff. I'm beginning to see that there's something in it."

"Of course there's something in it," said Costock.

"I wasn't brought up like you chaps," Longcroft said apologetically. "Perhaps I shouldn't admit it, but sometimes I feel sort of small, and out of place—as if I shouldn't be here at all. *That's* something you can't understand! I was brought up in mean streets, and by God, were they mean! But right from a kid this was what I wanted—to live in a nice little cottage in a pretty village. I wanted clematis round the door, and a rose garden, and a grass lawn. Well, I got 'em, but the only way I could get 'em was by turning a flair for inventing stories into a hard-boiled business. I learned how to string words together to describe the stories I saw on my mind . . ."

He looked round at Costock.

"I'm not satisfied with what I write, Mr. Costock, in spite of all our more or less friendly arguments, and I'd like to do better—but how the hell can I? I'm scared—scared, I tell you, of having to go back to *that*! You wouldn't understand it. You couldn't understand it!"

"Try living in a bed-sitter in Norfolk Square, and trying to write with your wife and kid over a hundred miles away from you," said Grayson in a quiet voice. "Try writing something decent knowing that your enemies and most of what should have been friends are talking about you! Grayson is finished. Sausage for breakfast, hot dogs for lunch, hamburgers for tea, and sausage rolls for supper. God, *don't* I understand!"

Longcroft nodded. "Yes, Mr. Grayson; you would understand, but you're the type that can accept it. You say it's all experience, and can be worked into a book, but your life didn't start like that! And that's why, to some extent, I could understand Moston. He came out of the back streets of Leeds, and found that money was the only key. And when he'd found the key, well, he turned it for all he was worth. And that's why I'm probably the only man here who wouldn't have killed Moston—because I understood him, and the rest of you never did."

Grayson gave a wry grin. "And what you don't understand you fear, and what you fear you kill if you think you can get away with it. Longcroft, you've turned the argument right back on us."

"Y'know," said Longcroft earnestly, "I've had a pretty good run in Wingford. You've all put up with me, and been real gentlemen—"

"Oh, shut up, Longcroft!" exclaimed Costock. "You'll have me in tears in a minute! You've always paid your score, and you've never scrounged. You're as good as any other man that comes into my house. I'm sorry if I ribbed you about your stories. They're good stories, otherwise they wouldn't have sold, and you're giving pleasure to thousands where I'm only giving it to hundreds."

"Always pay your score," said Longcroft. "Yes, that's what you have to do!"

Brother Ignatius touched Longcroft lightly on the sleeve. "Life is like good wine that is poured into a variety of vessels. If a vessel should feel that it is unworthy of the wine, then from that moment the virtue of the wine begins to enter the clay of the vessel, and the vessel becomes more worthy to contain it. It is only when the vessel feels itself worthier than the wine that the wine grows sour and breaks the vessel so that it may flow away in search of a worthier one in which it may regain its virtue . . ."

"As in Moston's case," said Costock.

Longcroft pulled his cloth cap over his eyes. "Thanks—for everything," he said, and left hurriedly.

Vere Bolding coughed loudly as Longcroft's footsteps faded in the passage. "For God's sake let's have a drink, Costock."

Costock looked down the passage. "There goes a nice little man—the silly clot!"

VII
Pattern of Battle

GRAYSON AMBLED downstairs and into the kitchen shortly after half-past seven next morning. Costock was dashing to and fro on chores concerned with the business end of the house, and gave him but a friendly smile and a nod. Doreen was cooking breakfast. She greeted him with a friendly smile and indicated that he could take over the frying of the bacon. Grayson gravely considered the unusual size of the pan, and the amount of bacon in it. "Don't tell me that the chief suspect has to cook breakfast for the cops!" he complained.

"Good lord, no! They aren't even out of bed yet. That little ration is yours, and mine, and Mike's. Eggs to follow. Don't burn it."

Grayson skilfully steered and pushed the rashers round the pan with a fork, from centre to rim, and round and about, while from the corner of his eye he watched the trim efficiency with which Doreen prepared the table. He closed his eyes against the scene. It was one of the many domestic delights now missing from his life.

"Bran!" Doreen said after a time.

"Well?"

"*What* are you going to do about Corinne?"

"That's a good question," said Grayson. "You might almost call it the thousand-dollar question, but I doubt if I can think of the answer before the allotted two minutes is up."

"But something will have to be done about her, Bran!"

"Yes, if only for Nat's sake."

Doreen moved about the kitchen, trying to appear casual.

"Is it that way, Bran?"

"It's that way, Doreen."

"Don't you think, perhaps, that you're—well, taking too much for granted. Don't you think that present circumstances are producing present tensions, and that with time she . . . ?"

"You don't know Corinne, Reen," said Grayson. "It took me years to really learn anything about her. Truthfully, it was only the other night, at the bottom of Herby's drive, that I really saw her for the first time. Until then, despite eating and sleeping and living with her, she was always something beyond my grasp—like trying to know Nefertiti by staring at her picture. Then, when she faced me in the near darkness by the Lion Gates, it was as if I'd been taken back three thousand five hundred years to Akhnaton's city to see what had been a mere painted bust come to life. I really saw her then. She has the same cold intellectual façade as Nefertiti, you know, and I saw behind it for the first time, and all the clues I'd gathered through the years rushed together."

"And what did you see, Bran?" asked Doreen, while she continued to slice the bread as if the whole conversation was one of normality.

"She's like a cat, Reen," said Grayson. "I've always admired and loved cats. They are impudent, and aloof, and independent as Lucifer. But I can't admire those qualities in a woman, especially a woman who happens to be my wife. Yes, she's like a cat. She expects everything from life, and does not expect to give anything in return. Even Paul Longcroft has evolved higher than that!"

Grayson paused for a second, and then continued: "What did Descartes say? *Cogito ergo sum*—I think, therefore I am. Paraphrase that, and you have Corinne. *I exist; therefore I accept.* She has talents, but she'll not use them. Life has created her without her consent, and must pay her for the privilege. She can play a piano like an angel presumably plays a harp—with excellence, but she will only play when alone. She knows I love my Chopin above all others, but when I'm around she plays anything *but*—apart from the *Polonaise in A*, which I loathe because it sends disturbing trickles up and down my spine."

"Why did you marry her, Bran? Why did she marry you?"

Grayson shunted the bacon round the frying pan, and grunted. "Blessed if I know. That is, I know why I married her, but I don't know why she married me. Once Nat was born and in her arms she apparently had everything she wanted from marriage. She sat in bed with the baby in her arms and an enigmatic Mona Lisa smile on her face. It was then I realised that I was living with a stranger. It almost looked as if she had no will nor wishes of her own, but as if the life force was moulding the pattern, and having fulfilled the biological function of reproducing the species, it was satisfied.

"As a human being, and a writer, I knew women tended to switch their affections from husband to baby for a while. I was prepared for that, but she never came back. She tried to keep Nat for herself, but Nat and Nature were too strong for her to create a monopoly. Nat is now as much mine as hers."

He looked round at Doreen. "Ignore that possessive note. I don't mean it that way. I'm just fumbling for words. What I'm trying to say is that the spiritual link between Nat and myself is complete, despite Corinne's attempts at insulation."

Doreen crossed the kitchen, and leaned over him to get the boiling kettle. "You know something, Bran?"

"Such as?"

"In spite of the way you've just carved her up and dissected her, you still love her."

Grayson continued to steer the bacon round the frying pan, forming the rashers into triangles and squares.

"Yes," he said flatly. "I still love the wench, and I'm beginning to wonder if I should despise myself for my weakness. If I were a conventional type I'd go off to Africa and work off my frustrations by shooting poor lions that have never done me a ha'porth of harm."

Doreen laid an affectionate hand on his arm, and quoted:

"And of love I have this to say: that it is both bee and flower. It gives and takes the nectar that brews into honey. Woe to the one who separates the giver from the taker. Woe to the one who would replace either bee or flower. Upon his head all the sorrows of the world will heap. The nectar will turn into gall . . ."

"That's the motif from one of Konrad Bercovici's stories—'Muzio'," said Grayson.

"I don't want to go all sentimental, Bran, but you know that me and Mike love you—really love you?"

"Yes, and it humbles me," said Grayson. Then, almost too briskly, he asked: "What follows, my little cabbage?"

"For, great as is the sin of giving kisses to one thou dost not love, as great and greater is the sin of accepting kisses from one not loving thee."

"Well?" said Grayson.

"She might do it for Nat's sake—a sacrifice. You're still the breadwinner. I know you better than I know Corinne, and as love must feed on love you might feel so hungry that you mistake the shadow for the substance. Adultery is something you mustn't consider, Bran."

"I know," Grayson sighed. "I've already thought that out. There's Nat!"

"At the risk of sounding trite I must say that time has a knack of solving most problems."

Then she glanced at the pan, and sighed heavily.

"What's wrong?" asked Grayson.

"I think we should give that which is uneatable to the dog, and put fresh bacon in the pan. As firewood, or brandy snap, it would be perfect."

It was just after half-past nine when the ambulance hurried through the village, its tinny bell calling all the sixty Wingford housewives to their doors.

"Gone round the church," said Costock, putting his head into the kitchen. "We'll hear all about it as soon as we open."

But they heard about it shortly after ten o'clock, when Longcroft knocked on the back door and put his head into the kitchen where Doreen, Costock, and Grayson were having early elevenses. "Can I come in? I'm glad you're here, Mr. Grayson; it concerns you."

Doreen got out another cup and saucer, and Longcroft threw his beret on the welsh dresser.

"Who was hurt?" asked Costock.

"Coffee, Mr. Longcroft," said Doreen.

"Thanks, ma'am. It was old Mrs. Walters. Poor old girl's been whipped off to hospital. She reckons to come in and do for me round about a quarter to nine every morning. She hadn't shown up by ten past, so I trotted round the corner to see if she was all right-—and she wasn't."

"Do I know her?" asked Grayson.

"Bustly little body, always dresses in black, and usually wears her apron under her coat," said Doreen. "She's sixty-two, and dashes round as if she was forty-two. Used to be the only midwife for miles. Greatly prized was Mrs. Walters. Still, what happened to her, Mr. Longcroft?"

"No answer when I knocked, so I tried the door. It was unlocked, so in I went. The old dear was lying across the hearth, barely conscious. I rang for Doc Sleaford, and he belted straight out from Yeagrave in his car. So far as we can make out, she was cleaning her grate last night—she always lays it ready for morning—and slipped. She fell across the brass knobs on the fender. Got a bruise as big as a teapot in the middle of her chest, and Doc thinks she's done in at least two ribs. Risk of pneumonia at her age, he says."

"Poor Mrs. Walters!" said Doreen. "And lay all night without attention!"

"But I didn't call just to pass on the news," said Longcroft.

"For some queer reason she'd got you and your troubles on her mind, even when Doc was poking her chest and making her squeal. I was to give you the key of the cottage, she said. She didn't look like needing it for a few weeks, and you were to take your lovely wife and sweet little girl there and consider it your home. If she came back before you left, well, it wouldn't matter. There was room for all. She meant making the offer today in any case."

"It's nice of her," Grayson said slowly. "Very nice indeed."

"And she wouldn't be averse to a visit from you while she's in dock," said Longcroft.

"I'll take her some grapes and flowers."

"And now," sighed Longcroft, "I must hie me to Yeagrave. The Yard men want to have a talk with me on their own muck heap."

Grayson looked up quickly. "Why you?"

Longcroft sniffed. "Some Charlie or Charles has let it slip that I was in the vicinity of the manor at an inappropriate moment, and I have to explain my presence."

"Were you there?"

"Yes," he said simply.

"Why?" asked Grayson.

"Look, cock," said Longcroft; "the way you went out of here on Sunday night was the way gents where I was brought up went out when they intended using a razor for purposes it wasn't intended for. So I came after you, to butt in if you got on too intimate terms with Henry Moston. When I saw you performing in a gentlemanly if somewhat unconventional manner I scarpered back to my beer."

He gave a broad grin.

"And now I must be off to catch the Yeagrave bus. Thanks for the coffee, ma'am. See you all tonight, I hope." Costock watched him go, a thoughtful tongue in his cheek.

"The ass," he eventually commented.

"I don't get it," said Grayson. "You made a similar remark when he left us last night."

"You wouldn't get it," replied Costock. "You are still half asleep. Longcroft is going to pay what he considers his debt to Wingford. He knows one of us did Herby in—"

"One of *us*?" Grayson interrupted.

"I also was on the job," said Costock. "I suspect there were others. You didn't think I wanted you to land yourself in any worse mess than you were in, did you? Anyway, it looks as if Longcroft worked fast after leaving us. He's let it be known in some right corner that he was at the manor, and the news has conveniently got back to Knollis."

He shrugged, and passed his empty cup to Doreen for a refill. "Well, I suppose it will all help."

"I keep wondering where Brother Ignatius is putting himself," said Grayson.

"He's always been a mystery," replied Costock. "I don't know what he's doing. He's booked lunch for today and every day of this week, but beyond that he might be invisible for all I see of him at other times."

"But where is he staying?"

"I don't even know that. Excuse me; that's the sitting-room phone."

He came back a minute later. "Your agent on the blower for you—all the way from London Town. He has news."

As Grayson went out, Costock and Doreen sat silently; wife regarding husband quizzically, and husband grinning at his wife.

"Mike . . ."

"Yes, darling?"

"Mike—you didn't . . . ?"

"No, love, I did not kill Herby, but if the need should arise I shall let the tecs chase me all the way round England."

"I didn't think you did, but—well, you know!"

"I know," agreed Costock. "As a matter of fact, sweetheart, I had a grandstand view of the whole thing. Longcroft didn't see me, because I was in the shadows, but he was peeping through one hedge, and I was peeping through the opposite one. Bran made a good do of it!"

"Who *did* kill Herby?"

"I truthfully haven't a clue, Reen! Longcroft left shortly after Bran, and I followed Longcroft. He came in by the business entrance, and I went round the back to leave my coat and cap in the kitchen."

"Then it wasn't you, or Bran, or Mr. Longcroft. That's something to feel pleased about."

"It certainly wasn't two of us. The difficulty about Bran's tale of going for a walk is that of persuading Knollis that he really went all the way to Headley Corner—and as Bran doesn't know that himself it makes the situation somewhat complex. He could have gone back to finish off Herby as a sort of second thought—making sure that Corinne and Natalie had no more trouble from him. Between you and I and the gatepost his position is not exactly enviable."

"Poor Bran! He's having a lean time."

"Remember Pharaoh, sweetheart! He also had seven fat kine as well as seven lean ones."

"But Pharaoh got the fat ones first, and saved up against the lean ones. You can't do that with trouble!"

"Oh, well," Costock said carelessly; "everything will turn out well for him in the end."

"That's a good one for a master of tragedy," Doreen retorted. "You've never yet written a story with a happy ending, and now try to kid me that it's bound to come right for Bran. It's no good being merely hopeful, Mike. Or hypocritical—especially when you don't believe in happy endings."

"Life runs to patterns, darling," said Costock. "I rather fancy that Bran's will be a presentable one sooner or later. So far as my tragic endings are concerned, well, they are literary guile. If I twisted a climax the other way nobody would read me."

He broke off as Grayson burst into the room looking pleased with himself.

"What's to do?" he asked.

"Rosing's almost worked the oracle with the Metropolitan film people with two books—*Storm Bird* and *Latimer's End.*"

Costock whistled softly.

"If that comes off we're in the money. Nice folding lolly, followed by Brandreth Grayson being fashionable for at least three years. In two years I could buy Wingford!"

"What in God's name for?" asked Costock.

"I'd like Wingford," replied Grayson simply.

"Oh, well," said Costock, "every man's entitled to buy his own torture chamber if he chooses. In any case if Rosing works fast you should be able to tap the proceeds within a few weeks, and then you'll be back in a decent house with Corinne and Natalie, and all your troubles will be over!"

"How did this sudden move arise?" asked Doreen. "You have been trying to push the film boat out for over two years."

"We-ell, Rosing told me that there was a—well, shall we say a kind of sympathy with me over the crash. Some character of other up at the studios wondered if I had written any presentable stuff, looked into it, and then decided it might be worth cashing in on the publicity . . . if you see what I mean?"

"That," said Costock, "is as modest a collection of lies and understatements as has come my way in many years. Still, let it go if the results are satisfactory."

"Poor Corinne!" Doreen murmured. "She won't like it one little bit."

Grayson stared at her. "No-o, I suppose that's true, now you mention it. Despised husband proved worthy, and the day hastened when she has to share the same house with him once more. Which reminds me that I'll have to phone and pass on old Mrs. Walters's offer. She'll refuse, of course."

Corinne did refuse to return to Wingford and take temporary possession of the old lady's cottage.

"I've told you I'm not returning to you as your wife," she said. "Such a state of affairs can be easily concealed in a London suburb where no one knows, nor wants to know, anyone else, or anything about them. In Wingford—pff!"

"You hardly need worry about Wingford," Grayson replied caustically. "Everybody knows everything already. Blame your own indiscretion, and the natural curiosity of Alice Day and the other skivvies for that! At the moment the village would take little or no notice if you shared sleeping quarters with Brother Ignatius. The point is—Nat!"

"Natalie," corrected Corinne.

"She's my kid," said Grayson, "and I shall call her just what the hell I like. The fact remains that the longer she's away from me the worse she'll pine—"

"For *you*!" Corinne interrupted.

"For me," said Grayson firmly.

"Your sloppy sentiment makes me sick!"

"That makes a nice change, being accused of sloppy sentiment," said Grayson. "It's a change from being idle, worthless, and inconsiderate. And now I'd like a word with Nat if you don't mind."

"She's not about."

"That isn't true. I insist on speaking to her—"

The line went dead.

Grayson looked into the mouthpiece, and said: "Oh, well! There are other days."

He went to his room, and from the casement watched the many comings and goings of many cars to and from the manor. It seemed that Scotland Yard and the county police were going about the task of finding Herby's killer in the grand manner, much work and great trouble being of no importance. Meanwhile, Paul Longcroft—the silly clot—would be taking a hammering down at Yeagrave Police Station, now battle headquarters, and it would be interesting to hear his own version of the fray on his return, if he returned.

Longcroft did return. He arrived back at the Barley Mow at tea-time, and staggered melodramatically into the kitchen.

"Heck!" said Costock. "He's drunk!"

Longcroft shook his head. "Not drunk—frustrated. You can't make these London rozzers believe a word you tell 'em. I've been foxed, and I've been done!"

"Perhaps a cup of tea would help, Mr. Longcroft?" Doreen suggested.

"Make it in a bucket, Mrs. C.!" said Longcroft. He took off his hat and flung it behind the door. "Here's me, trained to make the Average Reader—blast his hide!—believe any fantastic story I like to invent, and I couldn't put a good yarn like that across a couple of dicks. Heaven help me, Aristotle! Cor!"

"Depends how fantastic the story was," suggested Costock. "I've read little enough of your stuff, God knows, but in the main it wouldn't deceive a boy of ten."

Longcroft held up a warning finger. "Ah! That's the point! Convincing a child is one thing. Convincing an adult is another. A child sees through lies and inventions! A child asks for every i to be dotted, and every t crossed. Adults just mop up stories. These Knollis and Ellis characters are just two simple leetle childer what don't believe a word anybody says to them. Cor, the questions they asked!"

He paused to accept a cup of tea from Doreen, and pulled his chair to the table expectantly.

"Mrs. Doreen, ma'am," he said, "if you've a very old slice of bread, and some butter that has gone reasty, it would come in useful to a man what has just been through purgatory."

"What is on the table is yours, Mr. Longcroft," said Doreen, "but leave that old crust for us. We'll share it later."

"Being serious," said Costock, "I'm interested in your serial. What the dickens did you tell them?"

"It wasn't what I told them, but what they made of it," replied Longcroft. "Tricky, that's what they were. Kept jumping from one subject to another, and then looping back again. And then, after the first hour, Knollis commented that I was one of the most interesting personalities he had met in a lifetime of investigation. Judging by his notes I was able to be in three different parts of the estate at the same time. He said he'd like me to meet him in London some time to be introduced to a friend who was a member of the Magic Circle . . . !"

"I've heard he's inclined to be sarcastic," said Costock.

"Two can play that game," said Grayson.

"You'll get the chance," said Longcroft. "They are gunning for you, old man."

"But I cleared myself!"

"That's what you think. Mind you, they didn't exactly confide in me—"

"Not to any great extent," interrupted Costock. "They only outlined the main plan!"

Longcroft shook his head. "Entirely wrong! But I did pick up certain casual remarks and piece them together. And in my youth I worked on newspapers and can read even shorthand upside down—"

He broke off suddenly, as if aware that he was saying too much. He looked down at his plate as he met Costock's eyes across the table.

"Having gone so far, my Philistinic friend," said Costock, "you had better go the whole way. You've given the man your coat, so give him the cloak as well."

"Yes, out with it," said Grayson. "I can take anything by now—I think."

"We-ell," Longcroft explained reluctantly, "it's that famous walk to Headley Corner. They seem to think you knew you were being watched, and cleared off in the direction of Headley, only to come back when you thought you could do him in minus witnesses."

"I wouldn't have had the time," sniffed Grayson.

Longcroft sniffed in turn. "Ellis's shorthand notes suggest that you only went in the *direction* of Headley Corner. I don't know! I'm only telling you what I saw for myself."

"And the suggestion is that you thereby produced what you hoped would be a suitable alibi," Costock said quietly. "Bran, you must walk very, very softly."

Grayson was a quiet man for a few seconds, and then he scratched his head, and gave a wry grin. "Oh, well, the publicity will come in useful, no doubt! I wonder if Knollis will accept five per cent on sales?"

"Ask him in the morning," said Longcroft. "According to his desk diary you're down for a visit at half-past ten!"

VIII
Conflict Internal

AT HALF-PAST TEN the next morning Mr. Gordon Knollis was both courteous and persistent, and the interview that began in Costock's sitting-room was transferred to Yeagrave Police Station at a few minutes after eleven, as being "more convenient."

"You'll feel better on your own muck-heap?" suggested Grayson.

Knollis ignored the suggestion. "In your own interests we should have a shorthand note of anything you tell me—"

"Which will be taken down in writing, and may be used in evidence," Grayson interrupted.

"That is the procedure only when the investigator has made up his mind to charge the suspect with the crime," Knollis said gravely.

"And an abstract from Judges' Rules," said Grayson. "I was forgetting my long study of procedure. In this case whatsoever I shall say will be transcribed to longhand, read through to me, and I shall be invited to sign it as a complete record of the proceedings."

"Roughly speaking," said Knollis; "that is the procedure."

So they went out to his car, and twenty minutes later were closeted in a discreet room on the first floor of the section house, while a police constable in plain clothes sat at a table in the corner trying to look as unconcerned and detached as if filling in his football coupon for the week.

Grayson repressed a smirk as Knollis got under way. It was a useful experience, even if it was not one he would have chosen involuntarily, even in the sacred cause of looking for local colour, and in due time could be worked into a book. For such experiences he employed a tape-recorder, a mental tape-recorder, one that could be played back when the occasion or the story needed it. Long experience had trained it to work without any conscious effort on his own part. It absorbed, leaving him free to attend to the matters requiring conscious attention. It was his subconscious mind, which he whimsically called "George."

"And then you walked across to the main drive, and on to Headley Corner?" said Knollis, glancing at the few notes he had taken at the Barley Mow.

Grayson shook his head. "Oh, no! I told you that I took the short cut down to the Priest's Walk, through the topiary garden, and out by the wicket gate at the eastern end of the front wall. And *then* on to Headley Corner, if you don't mind me knowing which way I went."

"But why go for a walk at all?" asked the slit-eyed and obviously puzzled Knollis. "Why not go back to the inn and have a celebratory drink?"

"They can't touch me for it," said Grayson happily.

"I beg your pardon?"

"A colloquialism," exclaimed Grayson. "Goodness, don't you know that one! Anyway, to descend from the colloquial to the sublime or police language—there's no law against going for a walk, is there?"

"No," said Knollis, "but there must be a reason for it. Everything happens or is done *because* of something!"

"That's what Aristotle said."

Knollis raised an eyebrow, and apparently decided to ignore Aristotle. "Only idiots do things without a reason. There must be a motive for all action."

Grayson grinned. "You've been reading too many books on formal psychology. One of the delights of this otherwise crazy world is doing something without any reason at all. I'm obviously, by your definition, a first-class idiot. I do things on the spur of the moment without asking my reason for any motive whatsoever."

"Like walking through the night!"

"Like walking through the night," Grayson agreed.

"But on this occasion—but first, you're sure you went all the way to Headley Corner? There is a point where a side lane shoots off at an acute angle."

"I went to Headley Corner," said Grayson. "All the way to Headley Corner, completely to Headley Corner, and to nowhere else but to Headley Corner."

"But on this occasion, when you walked in the night, perhaps you had a reason for walking—"

"To Headley Corner?" interrupted Grayson.

A touch of annoyance flickered across Knollis's graven features, and was gone in the same instant.

Grayson said: "To think, Mr. Knollis. To think, perchance to dream."

"About what?"

Grayson raised an inquiring eyelid. He sought his cigarettes and lit one before answering. "You should know enough about my affairs to agree that I had, and still have, plenty to think about."

"I could concede that," said Knollis. "The subject on this occasion was—?"

"Candidly, I wanted to decide, for the peace of my mind, whether I had bettered or worsened the family situation by doing what I had wanted to do for so long—beating up Herby."

"You turned back at Headley Corner. Surely you had not found the answer in the comparatively short time it took you to walk there?"

"Quite honestly," said Grayson, "it was the physical action of reaching the corner that convinced me that I was wasting my time. Headley Corner, in case you don't know it—"

"Which I do," said Knollis.

"—is where the road forks," Grayson went on imperturbably. "I stood there for a few minutes, with the lightning playing round the sky like a classic Greek accompaniment, and saw the two roads as symbolic of my problem. Not being able to make up my mind which way to go, on which side of the problem to come down, I returned to base, literally and metaphorically."

"I see," said Knollis. "You did not meet anyone, coming or going?"

"Nary a soul," replied Grayson. "The corner is an old gibbet site, and the people round Wingford shun it o' nights—except young couples."

"They find romance there," murmured Knollis.

Grayson smiled. "The reputation of the site probably gives the young gallant an excuse to put his arm round the girl, and the girl an excuse to nestle closer to her swain," he suggested.

"It was obviously a bad night for courting?"

"I wouldn't know," said Grayson. "It's many a long year since I engaged in the pastime, and my memory is short. There may have been a couple in a field gateway. I wouldn't know that, either. I wasn't thinking about young lovers, but about a long-married couple who had somehow or other got their signals badly crossed."

Knollis nodded as gravely as a Chinese mandarin doll. "Then there may have been a courting couple who saw you at Headley Corner! The number of such couples in Wingford must be low, considering the lack of population. Shall we say a dozen . . . ?"

"Going to instigate a house-to-house search for sweethearts and lovers, Mr. Knollis?"

"It could prove profitable."

"And what if the only couple in the lane that night should be defying the veto of parents, and won't come forward to clear me? Or if they are an illicit couple?"

Knollis tch-tched. "For your sake I hope they wouldn't prove to be reluctant lovers."

"I realise now," Grayson said facetiously, "that I should have left my fingerprints on the gibbet post, and my footprints in the quagmire by the horse trough."

"It could have proved useful," Knollis said in a quiet voice.

"In the meantime I remain First Murderer?"

Knollis shook his head. "A Probable Murderer, but not necessarily First Murderer nor First Suspect, Mr. Grayson. Actually, I don't think you did kill Moston. For you to kill Moston would have been—how do you writers phrase it? Out of character? You might have killed him in the heat of the *melee*, but my experience tells me that you are hardly the type to go back and shoot in cold blood a man to whom you had just given a good and satisfactory hiding!"

"Thanks!" said Grayson.

"And yet you had the best motive," said Knollis, "and you might have swung from one extreme of passion to the other, and gone back in an ice-cold mood to finish Moston once and for ever."

"That's an interesting point, Mr. Knollis."

"You have to remember, Mr. Grayson, that you *did* tell Moston, in front of his wife, and in front of your wife, that if he came between yourself and your little daughter you would kill him, and that he would die hard."

Grayson looked up into the grey eyes of Knollis, and his jaw tightened. "My wife confirmed that?" he asked harshly.

"I cannot answer that question, Mr. Grayson, not even with the best will in the world to do so."

"You wouldn't work on such a theory solely on the evidence of Moston's wife, and *only* his wife?"

"That is something you must decide, rightly or wrongly, for yourself, Mr. Grayson. I am hardly in a position to advise you," Knollis said with extreme politeness. "For the main issue—well, there are few more painful deaths for a man than being shot or knifed through the abdomen."

"*I* wouldn't wish such a death even for Herby," Grayson said solemnly. "Impalement, crucifixion, and flaying, were regarded as fearful deaths. Herby must have died hard!"

"But for drugs, he would have done," said Knollis. "I see you know something about the nature of such deaths?"

"I've read medical and forensic textbooks."

Knollis tip-tapped the end of his pencil on the polished top of the desk.

"It could have been manslaughter, of course," he said, squinting upwards at Grayson. "It could also have been suicide so commissioned as to hang his best enemy."

Grayson looked at his cigarette. It had gone out. He threw it in the ash tray. "How come, Mr. Knollis?"

"Suppose you really did go back," said Knollis. "Suppose Moston heard you on the gravel, and rushed out with the gun. Suppose you grasped it, and in steering the muzzle from your body completely reversed the gun, and in the struggle it went off?"

"I can't oblige," said Grayson. "I did not go back."

"Sorry!" said Knollis. "That could be one explanation."

"And the other, or others?"

"That Moston, by sheer superior strength, once the gun was reversed, forced himself over the muzzle so that as he leaned on you the triggers were forced back by your fingers?"

"It is utterly fantastic!"

"Yet both methods are to be found in the history of crime—and both are to be found in forensic textbooks, Mr. Grayson," Knollis said pointedly.

"I only have Glaister, and Kerr and Brend."

"Others are in the public libraries."

"I must take your word for that. My crime stories depend on psychological clues rather than blood and queer methods."

The mandarin doll continued to nod for a while. After a long and silent spell Knollis said: "You are an idealist, Mr. Grayson."

"Am I?" Grayson murmured dutifully.

"You allowed your domestic life to crash into ruins rather than sacrifice an ideal."

Grayson grimaced. "You make me sound like a hero. It wasn't that at all, Mr. Knollis. Actually, there were two ideals. That was the very devil of it. That's what no one but perhaps Brother Ignatius and my friend Costock can understand. It was the internal conflict—and it was sheer hell. I had the choice of being true to my family, or to my friend—and if I let down either I automatically let down the other."

Knollis interlaced his fingers and balanced his chin on them, his elbows planted firmly on the polished surface of the desk. "How did you resolve the conflict?"

"I saw," said Grayson, "that I couldn't be fair to my friend and my family at the same time. I saw my wife and daughter as one unit, and Dickinson as another. To let down Dicky meant letting down everybody else—or so I saw it, and even now I don't think I was wrong. *This above all*, and all that, y'know. If I couldn't be true to mine own self I couldn't be true to any man, woman, or child. So I stuck by Dicky, and my ship and crew all went down together. It's beside the point to say that Dicky went down as well, but if I had pulled out on him there would have been three of us safe in the lifeboat, thumbing our noses at him as he went down with the ship. Looking at it from a purely materialistic angle, the onlookers would have said even ruder words about me then than they have done since the wreck. No, Mr. Knollis, there are some things you just do not do!"

Knollis nodded his agreement. "And your crew?"

"The mate does not approve, but I rather fancy the cabin girl is secretly enjoying herself—providing the stay on the desert island does not last too long."

"And the captain?"

"A very lonely man, existing in that mental and emotional state which is neither happiness nor unhappiness, and searching for another ship. You've had teeth out under a hypodermic injection? For some time after you are just numb. Your mouth is in a queer state where there is neither feeling nor not-feeling—a state that can only be compared with non-existence. That is Brandreth Grayson at the moment."

A wry smile crossed his face. "But am I a man, or am I a mouth?"

Knollis near-closed his eyes, and leaned back in his seat to regard Grayson intently. "I've met two idealistic murderers in my time, Mr. Grayson."

Grayson smiled gently. "What is the correct thing for me to say now, Mr. Knollis. I didn't bring my idiomatic phrase book with me."

"The normal murderer apparently feels a deep satisfaction with his work—in cases of revenge and vengeance murders. It almost amounts to exultation—for a time. Then comes fear. You can sense it while talking to them, even before you have made it anything like clear that they are suspected of the crime . . ."

"And so . . . ?" murmured Grayson.

"The pure idealistic has an entirely different reaction. He is satisfied in his own heart that he has done something that badly needed doing, and he develops the martyr complex. He's content—and where there is content there is no fear."

"And I show no fear," said Grayson.

"You show no fear, Mr. Grayson," said Knollis.

He got up, walked round the desk, and opened the door. The long-forgotten constable in the corner folded his notebook, and capped his fountain pen.

"Thanks for coming to see me," said Knollis.

"I was brought here," Grayson reminded him. "I was quite comfortable at the Barley Mow—where the bar has long been open."

"We must look round for young lovers," said Knollis with a friendly enough smile.

"Or old men with young mistresses?"

"Or that!"

"Or young men playing the gigolo!"

"You think we shall find one or other of them?"

Grayson shrugged. *"Quien sabe?"*

"Exactly, Mr. Grayson. Who knows?"

Grayson ambled contentedly from the police station. The interview had been less formidable than expected. Knollis had used the foil rather than the bludgeon, and although he was as innocent as any spring lamb he had still enjoyed matching his wits against those of Scotland Yard.

Knollis had made one important admission after granting that the times he had been given were accurate, the time at which Grayson left the Barley Mow, and the time he returned. Between those times, Knollis had hinted, it was possible for

Grayson to have walked to the manor, beaten Herby, walked to Headley Corner, and then walked back to the inn. It was also possible for him, within those times, to have walked part way to Headley Corner, returned to shoot Herby, and only then returned to the inn.

It was indeed a great pity, as Knollis had said, that he had no witness to his arrival at the Corner. It meant that his every move would be watched, and the feeling of personal freedom which he so cherished would be absent, perhaps for days or even weeks.

He shrugged the thought away, looked right, left, and right again, and crossed the road to the point from which a bus ran once every hour to the coast, passing through Wingford.

When halfway across he saw Brother Ignatius pacing up and down the pavement in a contemplative manner, and hailed him.

"Having a look round the shops, Brother?" he asked.

The little priest looked grave, and shook his head. "No, Mr. Grayson. I have been to the hospital to see old Mrs. Walters."

"How was she?"

"I am not too happy about her condition," said Brother Ignatius. "She was barely conscious, and appeared to have difficulty in recognising me—which is unfortunate, to say the least of it."

"She'll pull round," said Grayson cheerfully. "By all accounts she's a wiry old bird!"

"We must hope that is true," replied the priest. "How did you fare in your interview with Gordon Knollis? Or perhaps I should not ask."

"Nothing to worry about, really," said Grayson. "He'd obviously like to prove—or disprove—my story of walking to Headley Corner, but I don't think he was fishing for anything else, not seriously, anyway."

Brother Ignatius regarded the toes of his black shoes with more than casual interest until the bus arrived. He ushered Grayson on board, and then took the seat behind him. Grayson found the situation amusing for a time, and then appreciated that both of them had plenty to think about, and the priest had sacrificed the conventions to the necessities of the moment.

His own mind was in a whirl, a perplexed conglomeration of facts and doubts and worries about Knollis, Corinne, Natalie, old Mrs. Walters, Longcroft, and Mike Costock. He needed complete solitude for a period of several hours while he ordered the skitterbug of his mind to quieten so that he could review each part of his complex problem in turn, and then relate the parts to the whole.

"The whole art of life is that of learning to see the correspondence between things," said a quiet voice in his ear.

"As a thought reader you're pretty good," Grayson said over his shoulder.

"It is not a matter of thought-reading, Mr. Grayson. At a time like the present we are both bound to be thinking on similar, if not identical lines. You agree?"

"As a matter of pure fact," said Grayson, "I was thinking of solitude, and considering the possibility of another walk—a night walk. I have to be alone for a time. I don't want, at this stage, to engage in the art of seeing the correspondence between things. I simply want a chance to think of many things one at a time, and clarify each in my mind."

"I would hardly recommend the idea of another walk, Mr. Grayson. Not just now, that is."

"Why not *now*?" asked Grayson.

"You must realise that you are being watched and followed wherever you go. Men of the county force are engaged in what is known as 'making observation' on you. Another long walk, with your rucksack on your back, might be misinterpreted."

Grayson shook his head vigorously. He was not with Brother Ignatius as completely as he should be. There were implications of which he was not aware, and of which he should be aware. Somehow he had to find the catch that when touched would release the springs of the dark blind that had fallen over his brain some days—how many?—ago. And the answer lay in solitude and silence.

"In the silence wisdom speaks. . ." he quoted aloud.

"You have gone some distance on the way to wisdom," said Brother Ignatius. "Perhaps after all you should take your walk—

remaining silent. If, of course, you had some legitimate destination which would satisfy the curiosity of the police . . ."

"To Yarmouth, to see my little girl," said Grayson.

"An excellent idea," said the priest. "I, too, wish to walk. Perhaps we could leave together, and on the way I could leave you in order to seek my own paths, for I also cherish silence. In it the voice of wisdom truly speaks, and at no time better—"

"Then the hour before the dawn," broke in Grayson.

"One such precious hour, and I think I can lift the blind that crept over my brain to protect my sanity when my world crashed at my feet."

"Would eleven o'clock be a suitable time at which to leave?"

Grayson nodded, and no more was said between them.

On arrival at the Barley Mow, Grayson went straight to the telephone and rang Yeagrave Police Station, asking for Knollis.

"Grayson here," he said abruptly. "I thought it wise to let you know that Brother Ignatius and myself are going to Yarmouth— walking through the night. I want to be alone to think, so you can call off your blasted watchdogs. I give you my word I'll be in Yarmouth sometime before noon tomorrow. You can find me at my wife's address, which you have. Good day!"

"And if he does not accept your word?" asked the little priest, now standing at his side.

"I don't mind providing I don't see anyone trailing me," said Grayson. "If I do there'll be blood and sparks on the Yarmouth road! And even the presence of your reverend self will not deter me."

Brother Ignatius grinned boyishly. "You may not think it to look at me, but I have more than a useful knowledge of the gentle art of judo. Nevertheless, I must remember to pack iodine, arnica, and bandages."

At eleven o'clock that night, with sandwiches and two flasks of hot coffee provided by Doreen Costock, they set off in the darkness through the twisting streets of the ancient village to the open road beyond, Michael Costock bidding them a sarcastic farewell from the doorway of his inn, and promising to stand bail for either or both before noon the next day.

"It's funny," said Grayson, as they plodded along the tar-macadamed road.

"What is?"

"The way we met, and the way I unburdened my troubles on you, and now the way we're marching together into the night. It almost seems we've been harnessed together in some queer way."

"Maybe Ouspensky and Lahsen were correct," said the priest.

"And we've lived this before? Gone through the past few days together at some remote time past?"

"It is not even necessary to imagine this joint experience to have been in the *past*," the priest said in the lightest of tones.

Grayson sighed. "You surely aren't going to suggest same further fantastic theory such as a series of lives working in reverse, are you?"

"Oh, no! Oh, no," said Brother Ignatius, "although time is the great enigma. Have you ever seen any experiments with subjects under deep hypnosis? I don't suppose you have. When the subject is taken into deep hypnotic sleep, and then told to go and see what is happening in some remote part of the world, or even to go back, shall we say, to Agincourt . . ."

"Well? What happens?" asked Grayson, as the priest paused.

"The answer is always incredibly the same. 'I do not have to go because I am already there.' The operator then suggests that the subject return with the information. The subject invariably replies that he *is* back--that he is there and here at the same time. The answer to the question that consequently arises is that the mind of man is omnipresent, or conversely that there is no such thing as time as we know it. So that this joint experience is always happening, or happening always, or just *is*."

"Which," said Grayson, "is about as clear as the bottom of a duck pond!"

"Yes," the little priest replied; "you are correct."

"Trouble is," said Grayson, "that we aren't as highly evolved as we'd like to think. When you come to weigh up the facts there is very little that we are capable of comprehending. We've means of perceiving light, and sound, and we can taste, and smell, and touch—and yet how much experience lies outside the range of these senses? At one end of the visible spectrum we can appreciate the electromagnetic waves we call red, and at the other end those we call violet. The waves don't stop at those extremes . . ."

"It is a problem," the priest admitted.

"Y'know, Brother," said Grayson, "when I was about twelve years old I used to have a dream which scared me stiff. I dreamt of a king's crown, and the tiny cross at the top was surmounted by another crown, which was surmounted by another cross and crown, and on and on and on into infinity."

"The dream of eternal regression," said Brother Ignatius. "You can reach the same feeling of despondency by throwing out your mind to the extreme edge of the universe and trying to imagine that outside is *nothing.*"

"It's the way to madness!"

"There is only one cure," said Brother Ignatius. "That is the acquisition of religious faith. That, or wisdom and understanding beyond any degree that Solomon could have conceived. As you say, the solution really lies in the incompleteness of our evolution. Now we see in a glass darkly."

"And yet if the theory of eternal recurrence was a fact, and our senses were developed to a sufficient degree, we should be able to see what awaited us tonight, and tomorrow, and all the days that must follow, and take suitable precautions. We don't know what we may run into tonight, nor what we may miss—"

Brother Ignatius interrupted him. "Look at the light on the tree tops. A car is approaching us from behind. I think we should step to the grass verge until it has passed."

"Probably a police car, checking on me," said Grayson. "Suppose we step behind the bushes, and keep 'em guessing?"

The little priest chuckled in the darkness. "It would serve Gordon right if we did. I told him I would be with you. If he cannot trust you, he should at least trust me, for I am one of his friends."

He halted on the road for a fraction of a second, and then tugged at Grayson's sleeve. "Yes, let us hide! Let us play hide and seek with them throughout the night. You know, Mr. Grayson, it may be wrong of me, but I am beginning to appreciate your somewhat unusual sense of humour . . . Yes, by all means let us hide!"

They crouched low behind the gorse bushes and watched a long sleek saloon sweep past, its illuminated police sign on the roof an unwinking warning to any wrong-doers who might be out on the roads.

"There will be little poaching tonight," said Brother Ignatius as the rear lights turned into two red eyes in the purple distance.

Such cars—or it may have been the same one—swept past them eight times between midnight and dawn, and each time the strange companions hurried to the shelter of the roadside bushes, and did not tire of the game.

An hour before sunrise Brother Ignatius touched Grayson gently on the arm.

"This is where I leave you. A path leads through this wood on your right. It leads to the edge of a small stream. Jump the stream, and go through the clearing until you reach a small prominence crowned by six beeches. Perhaps there you will find the silence you need, and within it wisdom and understanding. Together, as you already know, they prove an excellent balm for a hurt soul. In my own place I shall pray for you, and for your child—yes, and for your wife."

He paused hesitantly for a few seconds, and added: "You know, Mr. Grayson, of the three she is most in need of help and solace."

Grayson looked hard at him in the pearly light of the false dawn.

"Brother," he said accusingly, "you surely did not think I wanted to pray for myself, did you?"

Brother Ignatius lowered his head as if in shame. "May God forgive me, Mr. Brandreth Grayson, but I did think that!"

He turned suddenly, and almost scampered down the road,

a diminutive little figure in a black cassock and skull cap, an

enigma vanishing into the mysteries of the approaching dawn.

IX
Strategy at Wingford

THE GAME that had been good fun when played with the little priest was no game at all when played alone, and Grayson, when he thought about it, felt extremely self-conscious about the idea of dodging behind roadside bushes for any but natural reasons. Apart from which, he realised it was definitely dangerous to avoid the police when he was only too obviously suspected of Herby's death. So that when his hour of meditation was over he went back to the main road and walked at an even pace on the last stage of his journey.

It was on the outskirts of Yarmouth that he came upon a stationary police car, over the driving wheel of which drooped a large black walrus moustache.

"Good morning, Sergeant Ellis!" Grayson said quite breezily.

"Morning, Mr. Grayson," said Ellis. "As my sole job in life is offering you lifts, perhaps you would care to accept one into town?"

"That depends on your destination."

"Your wife's present address. Where she is living with Aunt Florrie—from whom heaven protect me!"

"Why that?" asked Grayson.

Ellis sniffed. "She's the rabid Christian type who talks too much, does nothing about her Christianity, and has me crawling up the wall under five minutes."

"I've never experienced that aspect of her," said Grayson, "but then I've only seen her three times for periods of less than half an hour."

"You have much to learn," said Ellis gravely. "But about this lift?"

"We aren't going to the police station?"

Ellis shook his head. "In northern language, we are going to Ant Flurrie's."

Grayson climbed into the car and was whisked through the near-deserted streets to Aunt Florrie's house at the far side of the town.

Ellis brought the car to the edge of the kerb, and leaned over Grayson to open the nearside door. "I'll wait your pleasure," he said. "I don't think you'll be long."

"There's a mystery here," said Grayson.

"I'll wait," said Ellis.

There was something sombre, almost foreboding, in his tone and manner, so that Grayson went hesitantly across the pavement and up the six stone steps to the front door. It opened as he approached, and Corinne faced him, pale-cheeked and moist-eyed.

"What have you done with her! Where is she!"

Then she was beating her fists against his chest, while he tried to hold her wrists and shake her into coherence.

"What are you talking about?" he demanded. "Where is . . ."

He released her wrists, and his own arms fell uselessly at his sides. "You don't mean something's happened to *Nat*!"

The car door slammed, and Ellis joined them.

"Your kiddy vanished from the house shortly after eleven last night, Mr. Grayson. Three of us in cars have spent the night trying to find you and the parson fellow. We found him an hour after sunrise, sitting on a milestone, chewing bacon sandwiches. He had no idea where you were."

Grayson gave a bitter laugh.

"So it's funny! It's funny, is it!" shouted Corinne, and came at him again with clenched fists. Ellis stepped in between them.

"We shan't get anywhere this way, ma'am. Is it funny, Mr. Grayson?"

Grayson shook his head. "No, not funny, but neither of you would understand if I did try to explain. There's one thing, Corinne. I haven't seen Nat, and have had no part in her leaving this house. You say she left just after eleven? Where's Florrie?"

Corinne shook the angry tears from her eyes. "Having the vapours in bed—where it's comfortable—and praying."

"She could be doing worse," said Grayson. "Now shut up for a minute, both of you, and let me think. She vanished after being put to bed?"

"She was in bed by half-seven. Oh, Bran, you will find her for me!"

"I'll find her for both of us," he said dryly.

He dropped his hands on his wife's shoulders. "Did you bring all the personal luggage from Wingford?"

"How the hell could we? I'd packed most of the stuff by the time Herbert was found, and as soon as the police had done with us the next day we got out as fast as we could."

"Nat got all her toys?"

"Of course not. I had to concentrate on *essentials*."

"You brought Teddy?"

"Yes."

"And her Elizabeth?"

"No. She wouldn't pack very well, so I left her." Grayson gave a gesture of impatience at the same moment that his wife gave a gasp of understanding. The expression in her eyes could have been one of a newly-born respect for her husband.

"Has anyone looked for Nat at Wingford Manor?" Grayson asked Ellis.

"Not so far as I know," said Ellis. "Why?"

Grayson turned back to his wife. "Is Teddy missing?"

"I—I don't know!" Corinne stammered.

"Then find out," Grayson said calmly.

Corinne hesitated for a second before speeding up the stairs. She was down again almost immediately, breathless. "He's not there!"

"Then," said Grayson, "the father who does not understand his own child—quote—can tell you where she is." He looked at Ellis scornfully. "Detectives? I've—oh well, skip it. There's a lady about."

Ellis moved to the stairs, perched himself on the third tread, lit his pipe, and watched with interest as Grayson stepped to the telephone and rang Costock.

"Mike," he said, "Bran here. Nat has vanished from Yarmouth. Be a good chap and get out your car and slip up to the manor. You'll find Nat, and Edward Bear, and the doll Elizabeth in the golden bed in the east wing. Take charge of her, please. Then ring back to settle Corinne's fears."

He balanced himself on the edge of the Victorian hall-stand, and lit a cigarette. Corinne backed to the opposite wall and nervously pecked at her nails as she waited.

Costock's call came twenty minutes later, and he was in a facetious mood. "We've got her with us," he announced. "As forecast in our earlier issue, she lay in the golden bed with Teddy in one arm, and Elizabeth in the other, and was sound asleep. I carried her down to the car, and Doreen hugged the bear and the doll to her bosom and shed silent tears as she brought up the rear, and the beautiful little infant is in our own bed, and has not yet awakened."

"Hardly surprising, considering she walked through the night from Yarmouth!" said Grayson. "That is unless she got any lifts—which is more than I did by taking another route. Anyway, thanks, Mike. We'll be seeing you!"

He turned to Corinne. "Sergeant Ellis, the lift expert, will run you back to Wingford, and Mike and Doreen will look after you. It might be as well to take your luggage and consider Mrs. Walters's offer of the cottage. I rather fancy that our offspring has taken a fancy to Wingford Manor. I must remember to buy it when Herby's safely interred and Gwen beats it to the bright lights of London Town!"

"You coming with us?" asked Ellis.

It was a lightly veiled order, and Grayson knew it. "No," he said firmly. "I'm not—yet!"

"We'd like your company, Mr. Grayson!"

"What do you think I am?" demanded Grayson. "A bloody yo-yo dancing on a string organised by Scotland Yard. I'm going back to Wingford when I'm ready, Mr. Ellis!"

Corinne turned to him. "Bran! Please! *I* want you to come, too!"

"You've left it a little late, Mrs. Grayson," he said bitterly.

Ellis said: "Where might you be going, Mr. Grayson—if such a question isn't an intrusion on your so obviously treasured privacy?"

Grayson looked straight into Ellis's dark-browed eyes. "I'm going to eat breakfast at some cafe or other, and then I shall catch a bus back to Wingford. You needn't be afraid! I shall go back to Wingford, for I've things to attend to there, but it just happens that I'm getting choosy about my riding companions."

"But, Mr. Grayson . . ."

"Go to blazes, Sergeant," said Grayson.

Corinne said feebly: "Bran . . . !"

He ignored her, and walked from the house, fully aware that Ellis was moving over to the telephone behind the front door. He snatched his rucksack from the front seat of Ellis's car, slammed the door, and set off down the street.

He walked on, and in the centre of the town found a small and comfortable-looking cafe preparing for the day's work. He chose a seat in the bow window, and ordered bacon, two eggs, fried bread, and a large pot of tea.

"And I can wait," he told the sleepy-eyed blonde waitress. "I've the whole of eternity before me—and don't much care for the prospect!"

He lit a cigarette, and watched with mingled annoyance and amusement as a long, official-looking car drew up against the opposite kerb, and braked.

He left the cafe and went across the street to the car, in which sat two men wearing grey trilby hats, large men with keen eyes who could be no other than policemen; it was written all over them.

"Strangers in town?" he asked conversationally through the lowered side window.

"We're not," said the driver. "Why?"

"Just trying to help," said Grayson. "You've stopped under a no-parking sign. Not liking the police over much I thought I might save you the annoyance of getting a ticket."

"We're all right here," said the driver.

Grayson nodded, and thoughtlessly flicked his ash inside the car.

"Policemen, obviously," he said. "No one else would try such a silly caper."

"We are police," said the driver's companion.

"Now listen, my elementary friends," said Grayson, leaning negligently on the driving mirror. "I've eaten nothing but sandwiches for something over twelve hours—I think—and I fail to see why the good meal now being prepared for me should be eaten in the presence of my enemies. I fail to see why every mouthful should be spoiled by seeing you characters over the top of my fork. So I suggest you either join me at breakfast, or push off out of sight. I intend staying in the caff for at least half an hour. Then I shall go to a wash and brushupery for approximately fifteen minutes. After that I shall take a bus back to Wingford, if one is available. If there isn't, I shall variously walk and hitch-hike, and you can follow in third gear all the way if you wish. But I intend to eat my breakfast in peace!"

"You're doing yourself no good, Mr. Grayson," said the driver's companion.

"My deductive friend," said Grayson, "my world has gone so completely haywire that I can't do myself much more harm, so if you insist on watching me eat I shall risk a summons for common assault or mayhem by coming across and pouring the contents of the teapot down your neck-hole."

"That is threatening language!"

"Exactly," said Grayson. "I am suspected of murdering my unrespected brother-in-law. Well, you generally like to codge up some holding charge or other, so I suggest that—-when I've broken my fast—you take me in on a charge of threatening the police. I shall not resist. A few hours in a cell would give me a much needed respite from the excitement in the big outside world."

The two men exchanged glances, and the driver said: "clear off, Mr. Grayson!"

"No," said Grayson; "you clear off. If you don't, I shall ring your chief constable or great white chief and report you for parking in a prohibited place."

The driver leaned forward and turned the ignition key. "Mr. Grayson, I don't think I can learn to love you!"

"I'm not a bad character under normal conditions," said Grayson, "but just now, after losing my home, my wife, my child, and being accused of murder, well, I'm not exactly at my best! You've one minute."

The driver gave him a queer look which might have signified almost anything, and drove away.

"I'm in a most un-Grayson-like mood this morning," Grayson said aloud to himself, "but something attempted, and something done, has earned a slap-up feed."

He went back to the cafe, and when he eventually left he slapped his pullover, satisfied that he had put a good four-shillingsworth under it. He pretended to not-see the man standing opposite who slid a little too discreetly into the nearby telephone kiosk and pressed the emergency button.

He found his wash and brush up, and had a shave and a welcome swill. He asked the way to the bus from the attendant, and now beginning to feel fatigued he ambled slowly to the bus which would take him back to Wingford.

Aboard the bus, and his pipe going well, he smiled wryly to himself. He seemed to be doing everything he should not do, and to be wasting a lot of time that might be usefully employed. The night walk had been taken in the hope that he could remember exactly what he had done after thrashing Herby. Had he walked all the way to Headley Corner and back, or not? He remembered giving an answering goodnight to someone who spoke to him just outside the manor grounds, and he seemed to remember it was a woman's voice that came to him through the darkness, but nothing was certain.

That his mind—or his brain—was out of gear, was obvious to himself. He realised now that he had shot the whole story to the gang in the Barley Mow smoke-room, and had not been aware at the time that he was doing it. Overwork, anxiety, and worry had overloaded him, and it seemed that Nature had from time to time switched off his brain in order to save his sanity. To get back to normal he must relax, mentally and physically, and give his thinking apparatus the chance to work properly and clarify the experiences of the past few days.

He dozed off, and sank into a deep sleep from which he had to be aroused by the bus conductor when they came to the stop at the end of the branch road leading into the village.

"Police must be watching somebody for this murder," the conductor said conversationally as Grayson swung his rucksack from the platform. "Ruddy police car trailed us all the way from Yarmouth. Wonder who they want!"

Like Mr. Oakhurst, on the day he was to be turned out of Poker Flat, Grayson replied modestly: "Likely it's me!"

"You—a murderer!" exclaimed the shocked conductor.

"No, my friend. Nothing so famous. I'm only First Suspect. The murderer is still unknown."

As he walked into the Barley Mow he found everybody who was anybody waiting for him in the smoke-room. He looked round them sarcastically. "Welcome-home committee, eh? Knollis, Ellis, friend Michael, Longcroft the Philistine, Colonel Harry Vere Bolding, also of this parish, Mr. Crewley, and my darling wife. Well, well, well!"

"So you've arrived," said Knollis.

"You wouldn't like me to add the gag to the effect that to prove it I'm here, would you?" asked Grayson. "Thanks for the welcome, but I'm going to bed. It's days since I had a decent sleep, and now I'm going dead for a few hours. Although so early in the day I'm saying goodnight!"

Corinne reached out a hand to him. "But Bran—"

Grayson pulled his weary shoulders straight and square. "Listen, the lot of you! I've had enough. I've lived my life to a code, to a philosophy. That won't mean anything to convention-al souls who do only what is seemly so to do—for the looks of the thing and for face-saving. During the past few weeks I've been kicked and buffeted about from sunrise to bedtime, and taken it all without complaint. But now, I'm tired, and I don't think I'm strong enough to be weak. I tell you I'm going to sleep! But when I wake I'm going to take certain persons by the scruff of the neck and rub their noses in the truth, the whole truth, and nothing but the truth!"

"Bran," Corinne said quietly. "Mike has news for you."

"I couldn't care less."

"The film rights, Bran!" said Costock.

Grayson looked at Costock, and then at his wife.

"I see," he said slowly. "I'm coming back into favour again. I'm going to be Sound, eh? I'm going to have a Good Sitting Down. Well, I don't want that kind of Sitting Down, thank you, so you can ring Rosing and tell him to refuse the offers. There's a genie, or a genius or something inside me, and I just want to sit and write as he dictates. I'm going to rent a gamekeeper's hut in the woods, and write, and write, and write, and the rest of the world can go clockwise or anti-clockwise for all I care. Costock can write the caviare stuff, and Longcroft the fish-and-chips. Me, I'm just going to write!"

He yawned, excused himself, and dragged his feet up the stairs to his room. He dropped the rucksack where he stood, took off his tie and boots, and lay across the bed with a deep sigh of content.

Less than five minutes later Costock entered, carrying two glasses on a tray.

"If I'm expected to apologise for disturbing you, then you've had it," he said. "Sit up and neck this with me."

Grayson lay with his hands under his head, and cocked an inquisitive eye at his friend. "What is it?"

"Sit up," said Costock.

Grayson rolled to the edge of the bed, and Costock seated himself beside him and offered a glass.

"Here's to!"

"To what?"

"Oh, to anything, or nothing," Costock said airily.

Grayson sipped, and then beamed. "Benedictine! Then here's to the monks who prowl the hillside looking for the ingredients. Lovely, lovely stuff. One day I'll buy myself a bottle, lock the door, and drink the whole blooming lot. Then dream of Paradise and houris and benedictine flowing from the water taps."

"If you like benedictine so much," said Costock, "it might be as well to have a little more patience and listen to Rosing about Metro's offer—which will buy cases of benedictine."

"He's phoned?"

"Metro will take both books on terms to be discussed, and want an option on future work. You stand fair to be well in the lolly."

Grayson nodded soberly. "I must make an effort to see Rosing very soon—if Knollis will only stop pestering me."

"Rosing did ask how you were fixed, and I told him the position was slightly difficult. He said to tell you he'll come up for the day."

Grayson squinted over the edge of his glass. "He must anticipate a good killing. Although technically employed by his authors, he has hitherto expected his mountains to visit Mahomet. Yes, it must be something pretty good!" Costock tapped the stem of his glass with his finger-nail. "Bit rough with Corinne, weren't you? Especially in front of company? Not like you, somehow."

"What have I to lose?" Grayson demanded roughly. "She's hardly been in the honours list for her consideration of me."

"She has taken something of a pounding," said Costock. "After all, she lost her home, and got bumped out into a not too-friendly world."

Grayson raised his eyebrows. "What do you think I've been doing all these weeks? Dancing round the maypole with a glass of gladness in my hand?"

"Somebody said something about gently scanning thy brother man, and still gentler sister woman. Now who was it . . . ?"

"Couldn't care less, frankly, Mike. Not in the mood for quizzes. Better try again when I've had some sleep."

"Your philosophy's slipping."

"I must use stronger elastic."

"And being facetious won't help matters!"

Grayson sipped slowly at his glass for a time.

"I wonder," he said, "if I really want matters helping. Brother Ignatius served up that facer to me on the train last Saturday. It was well wrapped up, of course. He went round it by considering the morality of intervening when he saw Brother Man and Sister Woman in trouble. He implied that the Rules of the Game—with capital initials—forbade intervention, and threw off the casual remark that at times he had failed to obey the injunction, or unwritten law."

"What would you do, chum?" asked Costock.

"Me? Oh well, in my present mood I'd see even my best friend fall off the end of the pier without lifting a hand to help him. He's entitled to jump off if he wants to do so. His life is not mine nor yours."

"What is life?"

Grayson hesitated, and again sipped slowly before answering. "Now there's a question. What's life! It's the stuff of the universe. It's the stuff that pushes up flowers, and shrubs, and trees. It sleeps in the stone, dreams in the animal, and wakes in man. It's the electricity stuff that makes us tick."

"You don't confuse it with God?"

"No-o," said Grayson. "It's of God, but not God. I'm explaining it back to front, but this is how I see it. There's a pattern of growth for everything in the universe, organic or so-called inorganic. Apart from sports and mutations, the cause of which no one really understands, each flower and bird will grow up pretty much like its forebears because it lacks consciousness, and therefore the ability to vary the pattern. It's in man that the bud of consciousness is beginning to open. Being conscious or aware, at least to some extent, of his potentialities, he can, again to some degree, direct the flow of life, because the stuff is completely neutral—just as is electricity, with which you can either electrocute a man in Sing Sing, or perm Doreen's hair. Which is the point! Control of it is the one gift God has given to man, and man has to take full responsibility for what he does with it. And that," concluded Grayson with a satisfied air, "is why I have no right to prevent my Brother Man jumping in the drink if he wants to do so!"

"If you saw Nat about to pick up the end of a live wire?"

"I'd snatch her away, or snatch the wire away."

"And that's where your temporary cynicism falls down," said Costock. "If you're prepared to save a child from its own ignorance you are also prepared to do as much for an adult. Size makes no difference. Neither does age, nor degree. So that, truthfully, you would try to save your friend from going to the devil in his own way. After all, that's more or less what you tried to do for Dickinson!"

"Oh, nuts!" said Grayson.

"And what you tried to do for Dickinson," said Costock, "you can do for your wife. You know that even after a few short hours she was being slung on the street by Aunt Florrie because her 'nerves' could not stand the strain of having Nat in the house?"

Grayson looked up, sharply. "She never told me!"

"The woman has her pride," said Costock. "They were moving to an hotel this morning if Nat hadn't solved the problem by sleep-walking back to Wingford."

"Sleep-walking!"

"Troubled sub-conscious mind," said Costock. "She cried herself to sleep wanting her Daddy. Then she got up and dressed and walked from the house, carrying Teddy. A lorry driver picked her up at the halfway mark. Still asleep, although her eyes were open, she told him she'd walked from Wingford Manor, and did not know her way back. He dropped her at the Lion Gates, and reported at Yeagrave just after we fetched her down."

"You know," Grayson said slowly. "There's something wrong with my mind. I never even asked after her, or for her, when I got back."

"You'd better have it," said Costock. "You are suffering from shock—which is why I'm so patient with you. In the last hour you've insulted all your friends—good friends who are trying to save you from the assize court."

"How can they help?" asked the puzzled Grayson.

"Time is the primary factor," said Costock. "It has to be proved, not so much that someone else killed Herby, but that you didn't. That is what we are all working on—for the murderer is somewhere hereabouts! So delaying tactics are being exercised.

Longcroft has been thoroughly grilled by Knollis because he deliberately put himself in the red. That gave us a full morning."

"Longcroft . . ."

"Heretofore the least respected of our literary clique," said Costock, "he is now the first to get his name on the roll of honour. He isn't really good at the game, but although Knollis chucked him out of Yeagrave Police Station as incompetent he probably held up the game for anything from one morning to twelve hours. Vere Bolding has now entered the lists."

"It's damned humiliating—especially when I'm as innocent as a spring lamb!" said Grayson.

"Crewley and myself follow Vere Bolding."

"Don't be a damned fool, Mike!" exclaimed Grayson. "Don't any of you be such fools!"

"Bran," said Costock slowly, "you said you spoke to a *woman* as you left the grounds."

"Yes, I did," said Grayson, and then paused and said: "My God!"

"They both have good alibis—at the moment," said Costock, "but meanwhile the hunt must go on. It's Crewley I'm afraid of, really."

"Why that? You don't think—?"

"I'm not at all sure, Bran. He's kept just that little bit too quiet. He was having a bad time with Herby, y'know. Treated like a dog, and Crewley comes of good north-country yeoman stock. While admittedly working for a living, and trying to make Herby's estate pay, he was not a money-grabber, and Herby was. While not in the Vere Bolding strata of society, he was nearer to pedigree than Herby, and having to work for Herby was a bit like a Samoyed and an alley-dog having to change kennels.

"Herby had been snarling at him too much just recently, and Crewley was on the point of rebellion. Full realisation of his own situation dawned on him when you came down and said that you'd been chucked out by Herby. I was watching his face and eyes."

He paused for a space of time, and then added: "In the darkness you might have mistaken Crewley's quiet and cultured voice for that of a woman. I don't know."

"What I can do shall be done," said Grayson softly. "Now clear out and let me sleep this evil from my soul. I'll be a new man when I awake."

Costock put the glasses on the tray and moved to the doorway. There he grinned. "In my house we expect gents to unclothe their bodies before getting into bed."

"I do that in decent houses," said Grayson. "In this case I shall put my boots on again before settling down."

X
Closed Ranks

GRAYSON AWOKE shortly after four o'clock, dreamily aware that someone was in the room. He shook the idea away, and turned over, drawing the sheet over his head. A soft breathing still reached him, so he turned back again and opened a cautious eye. Natalie was sitting on the foot of the bed, cross-legged, regarding him as gravely as a bronze Buddha. Grayson eased himself up and grinned sleepily at her. "Hello, Princess!"

"What's an unquest, Daddy?" she asked without preamble.

Grayson stretched his eyebrows, flexed his jaw muscles, and tried to think it out on Alice lines.

"Could be the opposite of a quest," he decided after a time. "A quest is when you go out looking for something, so an unquest would be when you didn't go out looking for anything. Where does it come from, anyway?"

"Mr. Burton, the policeman."

The light dawned on Grayson, and he nodded. "You obviously mean an inquest. What about it, Nat?"

"Mr. Burton's given Mummy a paper about you going to one tomorrow morning at eleven o'clock at Yeagrave Police Station."

"Should be an interesting outing," he said facetiously. "I'd rather go fishing."

"But you don't go fishing, Daddy!" Natalie protested.

"That, my sweet, is the whole point," said Grayson. "By the way, to save you asking the obvious question, an inquest is a meeting where a man called a coroner asks a lot of questions of many people in an attempt to find out how somebody died. In this case he is interested in Uncle Herby, late of this parish."

Natalie crawled along the bed to sit beside him. He put his arm round her slim shoulders, and she snuggled close to him.

"My nice Daddy!" she said, and immediately continued: "They should know that Uncle Herby was shot at."

"Yes, dear, that's true, but these things have to be done in what is known as an official manner—of which you'll learn plenty when you are grown up. It's good that they should too, because anybody can go to an inquest, and hear everything that is said, and also say what they know about what has happened, and then nobody can ever say that the truth wasn't told."

"Can I go with you tomorrow?"

"No, dear, you certainly can't."

"But you said anybody could go!"

"Yes, darling, but this is a grown-up job, and you wouldn't like it one tiny bit, anyway."

"My feet are sore, Daddy!"

Grayson squinted down at her, and wondered what to say.

"It's funny, Daddy!"

"What is, sweetheart?"

"I never knew before that you could walk about, and find your way, and not get lost, while you are fast asleep."

"Now who the—who told you that?" asked Grayson.

"I asked Uncle Mike how I got to Wingford, and he said he would tell me the Truth, since it never does anybody any good to tell lies, half-lies, or what-would-you's."

"This philosophic attitude towards existence appears to be catching," murmured Grayson to himself. To Natalie he said: "Well, if Uncle Mike has told you, that is that, and now you know that it is possible. Thing that's really puzzling your daddy is why you did it."

"I'd got Teddy, and so I'd got *you*," Natalie explained. "I hadn't got Elizabeth—and she's Mummy."

Grayson spent a time trying to sort out the application of Freudian identification. "But I was the one who was missing," he protested. "Your Mummy was with you."

The little head shook to and fro. "No, she wasn't! She put me to bed and caught the bus to Yeagrave. I was in bed by six o'clock," she pouted.

"Now there's a thing," said Grayson, and decided to change the subject.

"I dreamed that I went downstairs," Natalie persisted, "and Mummy wasn't there, so then I dreamed that I got dressed and walked to Wingford to fetch Elizabeth to love till Mummy came back. A man driving a lorry gave me a lift to Lion Gates, and it was all a very true dream!"

The door opened, and Corinne entered the room, poker-faced and angry. "I told you not to disturb your father!" she snapped.

Natalie nestled closer, and did not reply.

"She didn't disturb me. I was awake."

"That is hardly the point. I told her not to come to your room!" said Corinne.

Grayson kissed the top of Natalie's head. "You'd better go downstairs, Princess, and I'll climb out of bed and get all dressed up for tea-time. By the look of the clock I'll just about make it without upsetting Auntie Doreen's arrangements. Hop it!"

Natalie kissed him half a dozen times, and slid from the bed and round the back of her mother to the door, closing it after herself.

"I suppose she's told you," said Corinne, walking to the window and keeping her back to him.

Grayson dissembled. "Yes, she knows she was sleepwalking. I suppose Mike was right to tell her the truth."

"I don't mean that. She told you I went to Yeagrave?"

"Yes, she mentioned that in passing."

"You'll demand to know where I went!"

Although she could not see him, Grayson shook his head. "No, Corinne, I make no demands on you, now or forever more. You put yourself beyond requests or demands from me the other night at the bottom of Herby's drive."

"I've made inquiries about what I said, Bran."

"So what," he said shortly. He got out of bed and slipped into his dressing-gown and slippers.

"What I decided amounts to desertion. You can get a separation without any trouble . . ."

"Dear me!" said Grayson.

"And in three years you can get a divorce."

"Well, would you believe that!" said Grayson. "We live and learn, don't we!"

She swung to face him, her hands clenched behind her slim body. "Still the same mocking fool, with one face for the world, and the other for yourself!"

"I daren't show the world my real face," said Grayson, "and you've scoffed at what little of it you have seen in fifteen years. Let's cut the preliminaries—what are you asking me?"

"What you intend to do about me, of course. I must know what I have to plan for the future, for myself and Natalie."

"You've known me as a man for fifteen years, and as a husband for ten," said Grayson. "You should know what I'm going to do."

"You generally do . . . nothing. That's what makes me so mad at you. People talk, and people scandalise, and people libel and slander and tell lies about you, and what do you do about them? Nothing!"

"Exactly," nodded Grayson, "and that's all I'm going to do about you. The Chinese say that water is the most unresisting element in the world, and yet it gets everywhere and does everything. Gandhi more or less proved it. I'm an exponent of the policy of doing nothing. Let folk talk! Let 'em lie! Let them say what they want to say! They only hurt themselves, and they can't hurt me."

He took a cigarette from his jacket, hanging on the bed-post, and lit it.

"When we were married, Corinne, I vowed to take you for better or worse. I didn't crow when it was better—and by golly it has been better—and I'm not going to whine now it's worse. I stuck to Dicky on the same principle, and you've turned on me because of that, and now I'll stick to you. In cowboy language; ma'am, I ain't no piker!"

She propped herself against the wall and folded her arms. "You're an odd man, Bran!"

"Not being able to see myself objectively, I must take your word for it."

"What happens now?" asked Corinne.

"I'm still captain, even if the ship is lying at the bottom of the bay," said Grayson. "Soon, very soon, we'll have a new ship. Meanwhile we must bunk in temporary quarters, and I insist on having my mate and cabin girl with me. Tonight, after tea, we all three move into old Mrs. Walters's cottage, and present a united front to the world—and that is an order! What the situation may be inside is nobody's business but ours."

"There are only two bedrooms."

"Nat has one, you have one, and the captain sleeps on a coil of rope in the bilge. In this case it will be the sofa in the front parlour, in which I fully intend to work until three in the morning." He gave her an ironic smile. "You can put the back of the chair under the door-knob if you like, but I shan't bother you if you don't. Only two things in life interest me henceforth—Nat and my writing. Now as I don't like my housekeeper watching me undress and dress, perhaps you could go downstairs?"

Corinne moved reluctantly towards the door. "You pig!"

Grayson took her by the shoulders and pushed her out to the landing. "I'll be down for tea in just seven minutes," he said.

When he joined the party round the tea table he was surprised to see that Corinne's eyes were red, as if she had been weeping. Doreen, from the opposite side of the table, was regarding him balefully, and even Michael was in a subdued mood. The only cheerful member was Natalie, who sat next to him, and kept pinching his leg happily.

"That's the worst of not finishing library books before taking 'em back," Grayson said. "I'd only got part way through Dale Carnegie, and hadn't learned how to win friends and influence people—not in my favour, anyway!"

He flung his napkin on the table. "To blazes with it! I'll borrow your car and take Corinne's things to the cottage, Mike."

"I've taken 'em," said Costock. He hesitated, and then demanded: "Why the dickens can't some people behave like grown-ups?"

"Oh, but we do, Mike! We do! That's the trouble! If adults would only act like children there wouldn't be half so much trouble in the world. Ask Longcroft—he knows the answers. But no, if the game can't be played the way we want it, then we grown-ups pick up the football and take it home. We marry for better or worse, and while it's better we take it with both hands, and enjoy it, and praise the partner. But God help the breadwinner if they get down on crusts for a time. He is then the unprofitable partner who is cast into outer darkness.

"Do children play their game like that? Not until they reach adolescence, and stand on the threshold of manhood or womanhood. No, they kick and curse like little heathens, and the steam evaporates and they have their arms round each other's necks in less than five minutes. Children are honest with each other, and, more to the point, are not afraid of being honest with themselves!"

"Sounds like an epistle to the Corinthians," Corinne said scornfully.

"See what I mean, Mike?" Grayson asked. "I'm no angel—in fact I know I'm a most irrational character, a temperamental cuss who can be a darned nuisance to everybody at times, but I do try. Give me that: I do try!"

He left the inn and walked through the village to the constable's cottage. He was invited inside, and Burton said he was pleased to see him.

"Saves me calling at the pub in my rest periods," he said with a grin. "I never did like mixing business with pleasure, and now I can go for my nightly pint with a clear conscience."

"What happens tomorrow, Mr. Burton?" asked Grayson.

"Probably little or nothing, sir. If Mr. Kinglake calls you at all, which I doubt, he'll ask a few questions you've already answered on your deposition. You'll answer 'em again with what they call direct affirmatives or negatives, and after he's taken evidence of identification from Mrs. Moston he'll probably adjourn—as police request, pending further investigations."

"It's more or less a formality?"

"That's it, sir."

"Er—Mr. Burton. Do you think it would be all right for me to take a walk to the manor?"

"For why, sir?"

"Oh, I just feel like having a look round."

"Well," said Burton, "there's no harm in trying. If there's anybody there on the job, which I doubt, they'll give you a straight answer one way or the other. I think they've finished, and you should be all right."

"Thanks," said Grayson. "If Mr. Costock should pass over an unexpected pint or two don't think anything like—well, you know!"

"Thank you, sir," said Burton as he showed him to the door, "and good luck tomorrow—if you know what I mean!"

"That," commented Grayson, "is a sword with two edges. Nevertheless, thanks."

He took a short cut across the glebe to the manor, and crossed Peacock cautiously, looking anxiously ahead to make sure that none of the Scotland Yard men was about. He was not afraid of them, but preferred to make his visit to the gun-room without onlookers or escort.

He tried the main doors, found them unlocked, and let himself in. He made his way down the long corridors to the west wing, and so to the gun-room. He closed the door gently behind him, and looked round.

So this was where Herby had died. It was odd that a man who didn't know one end of a gun from another should die of one. Perhaps after all there was a destiny that shaped our ends— an ironic one in Herby's case. He had wanted to have round him all the accoutrements of a country gentleman, and when he had got them he couldn't use 'em, neither the provender nor the accoutrements, and was held in scorn by his man servant and his maid servant and the strangers within his gates.

The door swung open, and Gwen, dressed in widows weeds better designed for effect than mourning, was standing beside him.

"Come to look at the scene of your triumph, Bran?" she asked. "They say that murderers always return to the scene of the crime."

"I whipped him, Gwen, but I did not kill him," he said gently. "In your own heart you know that to be true."

"I'd like to believe it, Bran. I'd dearly like to believe it."

"I've never told you lies," he said. "Even when my ship was going down I told the truth to you and Corinne. I even told the truth to Herby, knowing full well that being Herby he would use the information to harm me."

"That's true," Gwen said in a voice that was almost a whisper. "Yes, Bran, that's true. You know, you should have married me instead of Corinne. You and I could have gone places. And yet you're a very odd man!"

"So your sister told me not two hours ago. I'm an odd man because I try to live straight—even if I don't manage it, which I don't, not by long chalks."

"Bran, who did kill Herbert?"

Grayson shook his head. "I don't know, Gwen. I wish I did. If Knollis and company don't find the character very soon I look like finishing up behind bars. I'm still the chief suspect because I can't prove that I walked all the way to Headley Corner and back after the rumpus with Herbert."

"Who could have *wanted* to kill him, Bran?"

"Perhaps nobody did kill him, Gwen. Perhaps it just happened. It could have happened when he and I got to grips, because he had the gun in his hands then. I twisted it away from him, and threw it aside, but if it was loaded then, and if a finger had got twisted inside the triggers, either of us might have got it then."

"I'd like to think that," she said. "I'd like to think it was an accident, and that he wasn't hated enough for anybody to want to shoot him. He was very good to me."

"Herby and I didn't understand each other," said Grayson. "It wasn't one-sided by any manner of means. It was oil and water not even trying to mix, and all the scientific processes in the world couldn't have emulsified us."

"Why are you here?" Gwen asked curiously.

"I wondered if there was something that Scotland Yard might have missed, but there isn't."

He led the way back to the great hall.

"You'll be at the inquest with us tomorrow," said Grayson. "Have you any message for Corinne?"

"There's no point in sending one to her, Bran, because she'll never forgive me for not intervening when Herbert sent her away. I tried to remain neutral, but I made a mistake, for both of them despised me for my silence. I was afraid of Herbert sending me away with her if I tried to protect her, and I didn't want to lose all this—and now I've lost it anyway, because I can't live here alone."

She grimaced.

"Funny, that! I always intended that Natalie should have Wingford when Herbert and myself were gone. Even he agreed to that as we had no children of our own—with the sole proviso that the gift was tied up so tightly that you couldn't get your hands on it!"

"She might get it yet," said Grayson. "I may be in a position to buy it shortly."

Gwen's head came up quickly, and she fixed him with an incredulous stare. "You mean that you really were speaking the truth—I mean about everything being in the bag, and it being only a matter of time before you were on your feet again?"

"Odd, how people don't believe you when you tell the cold truth," said Grayson. "So you thought I was romancing!"

"We-ell, trying to make the best of a bad story. We all try to save face, don't we? And it was true!"

"It was true."

"And you may be able to buy Wingford!"

"Providing I can raise a mortgage on it, I might manage it within two months—perhaps less."

There was a deep silence between them for a time, and then Gwen said: "Bran, I'll bargain with you . . ."

"This is going to be good," he replied.

"Cut out the Grayson sarcasm," she said. "If you'll promise to will Wingford to Natalie as soon as it is yours—in trust until she's twenty-one in case anything happens to you before then—I'll withhold the sale for two months and then sell it to you for the lowest price I can afford." Grayson looked at her quizzically, and somewhat doubtfully. "That's a stupendous offer, Gwen!"

"I'm a stupendous person, Bran. In any case, it's for Natalie's sake, and not for yours, so don't let us get our messages mixed. Neither, I might add, is it for Corinne! That might sound hateful to you, but I'm being fair, and playing you with the gloves off."

"I suppose I should accept," Grayson said slowly.

"There's one other condition."

"Press on regardless," he said cheerfully.

"You are never to let Corinne know the truth about the transaction. She's to think you got it at the price I shall ask by virtue of your own brains and business ability."

"That doesn't sound exactly honest," said Grayson.

An unexpected sneer came over her features. "It isn't, Bran! Of course it isn't, but then we two understand each other, don't we?"

"Do we?" Grayson asked wonderingly.

"Every man has his price, Bran. I estimated you rightly all along. You want to regain Corinne's good opinion of you, and retain Natalie's. I've shown you the way to do it—and I foot the bill."

"But—er—why? Might I ask that?"

"I shall foot the bill, and in return I shall have the satisfaction of knowing, for Herbert's sake, that he was right when he said you were a two-faced hypocritical no-good."

Grayson stared down at her again.

"You bitch!" he said without malice. "So that's why you've been so sweet to me over the last half hour. Leading me on, eh?

Well, you can stick to your estimate of me, Gwen, but not even for Natalie would I take on a contract of that nature."

"You can have Wingford at half the market value," she said quickly and almost desperately.

"Free of obligation, yes. With obligation, no!"

She hurried to the great oak doors and flung them wide. "Get out—you murderer."

"This must be something of a record," Grayson said as he strolled to the doorway. "Chucked out by both husband and wife in less than a week. There's only one thing I regret about this visit, Gwen—that I'd hadn't a tape-recorder with me. I could have played it over in my old age when I'm feeling low and something of a miserable sinner. It would have cheered me up no end!"

He passed her without looking into her angry and mortified eyes, and strode across Peacock to the main drive.

On the main road he saw Harry Vere Bolding ahead, and strode out to catch up with him.

"Pity I didn't fall in with you or somebody else on Saturday night," he said by way of greeting. "I might have been in an easier frame of mind by now."

"Not to worry, old man," said the colonel, flourishing his ash stick. "I have an early-morning appointment with your friend Knollis tomorrow. For some reason best known to himself he wants to know where I was and what I was doing during certain times on Saturday evening. Then comes the inquest, which I shall possibly attend as an interested spectator . . . depending on Knollis's reactions to my story . . . and in the afternoon friend Crewley goes to the inquisition owing to some weird idea or other that has got round to the effect that he also left the Mow shortly after you did so. Rather an interesting mass exodus on Saturday, was it not?"

"It must seem so to Knollis," Grayson said dryly.

"The man's full of interest and zeal," said Vere Bolding. "Looking forward to the affair, actually. Shan't have had so much fun since the Kaiser's war, when I was captured by the Bosche, and they wanted me to confess to being a spy for King George, and the President of the French Republic and the Czar of all the Russias or somebody. Although speaking German fluently in those days I professed complete ignorance of everything, including my mother tongue, and they finally drafted me into a most comfortable hospital as being *non compos mentis*. Heigh-ho!"

"Which won't happen to you on this occasion," Grayson assured him. "If you aren't guilty of anything they just turf you out on the street and leave you to get home as best you may."

"Going to shake 'em, old man," said Vere Bolding airily. "Going down in the old dog-cart. Had it cleaned specially. I shall drive up to the police station door, and they'll have to put a bobby on fatigues, horse minding. Good idea, eh?"

Grayson gave his first open laugh for days, and as soon as they entered the inn he ordered drinks round the smoke-room, where the usual company had assembled, not forgetting the enigmatic Brother Ignatius.

Costock beckoned him to the hatch.

"All your stuff's now at the cottage, in the front parlour as requested. Nat says to go up and kiss her whether she's asleep or not—and she will be! The kid's still very weary. You did say all round the room?"

Grayson nodded, and went to the corner seat. Shortly after ten o'clock he went to old Mrs. Walters's cottage. He tiptoed to Nat's room, and lightly kissed her curls. Corinne's door was closed, and he moved as quietly as possible past it, and down the stairs again to the parlour.

His supper was laid out on one corner of the table, and covered by a napkin. The kettle was singing on the edge of a low fire, and in the hearth stood the teapot, all ready for him as it had been in past times when he intended to work through the night.

He took off his shoes, and drew up a low stool. For a long time he stared into the flames, and then glanced guiltily at the table, where his work lay, and his typewriter stood ready for work, with a sheet of quarto and a backing sheet tucked behind the platen.

He made a pot of tea, and nibbled at the bread and cheese and bakewell tarts that had been laid for him. He drank three cups of tea, thumbed his nose at the typewriter, and went over to the sofa, where a bed had been made up for him. He undressed, and prepared for bed.

As a last thought he went round the table to take the paper from the typewriter, so that it should not curl and be useless in the morning. It bore one line of typewritten words: "Don't tire yourself by working too long."

He switched off the light, felt his way to the window, and flung back the curtains. He unfastened the latch, and opened the casement, and stood for a long time looking up at the squat spire of the church, silhouetted against the purple of the late summer night sky.

It was going to be quite a day tomorrow what with one thing and another. In fact today had been quite a day in itself. If Ouspensky and Lahsen were right, and he had lived all this lot several times before, how he had reacted to the situation on previous occasions, and how it had ended, were neat little points for conjecture. But it didn't seem that all the taking thought in the world could help him to see even five minutes ahead of the present moment, so he threw off his dressing-gown and slippers and got into bed, knowing that sleep was the only sane answer to so many insane questions asked by the perplexed members of the human race.

XI
Stubborn Spearsmen

MICHAEL COSTOCK sent two messages to the cottage shortly after breakfast the next morning. One was to the effect that Doreen would care for Natalie while he would run Corinne into Yeagrave to the inquest, and the second one was for Grayson; there had been two phone calls which needed his attention.

Arranging for Corinne to meet him at the inn later in the morning, Grayson walked down the village and pushed his way into the inn kitchen with an *élan* which was natural to him, but which was only just beginning to return as the dark blind rolled back from its darkening of his consciousness.

"Much in demand, aren't I?" he asked. "Two characters wanting me on the phone, and the Coroner wanting me in Yeagrave. However, we shall pull it all into one day somehow or another—although my poor novel is horribly behind schedule, and must shortly have attention, for on it rests the fortunes of the House of Grayson."

Costock cocked one leg over the arm of his chair and half closed one eye, regarding Grayson patiently with the other.

"Rosing rang," he said. "He's spent the night at Bury St. Edmunds, and will be here for lunch. T'other call was from Cartwright and Boulting, the estate agents in Yeagrave in case you've never heard of them. They ask if you'd care to call on them, as they have a proposition which might interest you."

Grayson stuck his tongue in his cheek. "Sounds like another move in Gwen's game to further discredit me in the soulful eyes of my wife. Wonder what she's thought up this time—although it could possibly be a straight business offer, because on second thoughts I can't imagine a firm of estate agents lending themselves to monkey business."

"Another move?" Costock queried.

While Doreen moved round the kitchen preparing the coffee which was available throughout the day at the Barley Mow, Grayson related his encounter with Gwen on the previous night.

"Nice work, in a way," Costock commented at the end of the recital, "but you couldn't by any chance have swallowed your pride to convenience your ambitions?"

"Could you?" asked Grayson.

"No," Costock admitted, "I couldn't. By the way, I tried to pump Rosing, but it was evident that what news he brings of treasure is for your private ear. While he wouldn't come clean with me, he confessed he had a mighty interesting offer for you. Lots of lolly in it for all concerned."

Grayson grinned. "I can imagine Rosing using that piece of standard English!"

"As a matter of fact he said it was an offer from Metropolitan, and it should prove highly remunerative."

"That's certainly more like him," said Grayson.

"It's rather useful that Rosing's coming first," Costock said reflectively. "If he has anything really promising you'll be in a better position when arguing with old Coltness at Cartwright's. Coltness is really the firm these days. Cartwright died ten years ago, and Boulting's so old that he only manages to totter in about once a week, just to look round and get off again. Providing you can raise the deposit you should be in a fair position to bargain for the manor. Coltness is like most of us round here, not liking jumped-up and cultureless characters in the district. We're dam-awful snobs, I know, but Vere Bolding's attitude is pretty typical. Cheap gems in beautiful settings and all that . . ."

Doreen poured coffee, and seated herself in a chair by the fire. "Help yourself from the table, boys," she said, and then in a reluctant voice said: "Bran . . ."

Grayson smiled. "Here it comes, Mike! Whenever she uses my name like that there's always something coming up to the boil!"

"Bran," said Doreen, "did you tell Corinne about Gwen's offer?"

"What—me?" he replied. "I should like to see Corinne get her ideas sorted out, and the trio back together on a fair family basis, but I don't use cheap tricks!"

He shrugged. "In case she'd probably decide it was just another of my alleged inventions designed to blind her to the true facts of life. No, Reen, it may be developing into a personal cliché, but I insist that there are some things you just don't do."

"I see your point, Bran," Doreen said quietly, and got up to carry on with her work in the house.

Corinne and Natalie arrived just before half past ten, and Costock brought the car round to the front door. Corinne elected to ride in the rear by herself, so Grayson joined Costock and helped him to drive, or tried to restrain him from driving in the mad way which usually endangered no one but himself. In spite of such help, Costock got them to Yeagrave well before eleven o'clock, and the three waited impatiently in the lecture-room at the police station which was to be used for the inquest.

Kinglade, the coroner, bustled in on the stroke of eleven, conferred in a whisper with Inspector Wing, who sat beside him, and then nodded to the policeman usher, who after three "O yea's" invited all who had business to do at this court before the Queen's Coroner, touching the death of Herbert George Moston, now lying dead, to draw near and attend.

The jury of seven men were sworn in, and then Kinglade stated briefly that they were there to inquire into the death of Mr. Herbert George Moston, and working from a statement too obviously prepared for him he sketched the known facts—the facts known to the public through the newspapers, and not the facts known to the police.

Gwen was called to the table, and sworn.

"You are Mrs. Gwen Moston, living at The Manor House, Wingford, and Mr. Herbert George Moston was your husband?"

"That is correct," said Gwen.

"Were you taken to the gun-room at Wingford Manor by Police Constable Burton at three o'clock on Sunday morning, and did you there recognise the body shown to you as that of your husband?"

"Yes."

"He had been in good health during the past few months?"

"He had—very good health."

"Had he on any occasion ever threatened to take his life?"

"Never!" Gwen said emphatically, and turned deliberately to look significantly at Grayson, who ignored her.

"He had no financial troubles, Mrs. Moston?"

"Good gracious, no!" she answered.

Kinglade thanked her, and she sat down.

Burton took up the story. He had been called to Wingford Manor by Mrs. Moston, who told him over the telephone that her husband was lying wounded in the gun room. She had already phoned for a doctor.

"I went to the house immediately," Burton recited, "and saw that—in my opinion—he was critically wounded. I put a cushion under his head, but did not otherwise touch him or disturb him, and neither did I touch anything in the room. I went to the house phone and rang Inspector Wing at Yeagrave Police Station."

The doctor was called next. Like all the other witnesses he had made a written deposition, and Kinglade picked an odd question here and there from it, and was doing no more than performing a formality.

Then he looked up and said "Mr. Grayson!" The usher also called "Mr. Grayson!" as if Grayson was several miles away instead of sitting under Kinglade's nose.

The inspector whispered in Kinglade's ear, and Kinglade smiled and waved Grayson back to his chair. "We shall not need your evidence at this stage," he said, "and it is my duty to warn you that you need not give evidence at this inquest if you feel that the evidence you would give might render you liable to be charged with an offence, or would prejudice your defence if you should be charged with any offence."

Costock leaned over and put his mouth against Grayson's ear. "Wing had an idea of charging you for common assault!"

Grayson whispered back. "It wasn't a common assault! Herby regarded it as an uncommon one!"

"Silence!" bawled the usher.

Kinglade then said, addressing the court: "I understand that police inquiries are still proceeding, and also that the pathologist's report is not yet to hand. I shall consequently adjourn this inquest for a period of not longer than two months. You will all be called when required. Thank you."

He shuffled his papers back into his despatch case and bustled from the court as he had bustled in, a busy little man with a great deal to do in the world.

"Well, well," said Grayson, "wasn't that worth coming for!"

"It might have been worse—much worse," Costock said laconically.

He turned to Corinne, sitting on the other side of him. "Care for us to call at the Falcon for one before we go back?"

"I can do with one," she said. "My nerves are in rags after that flop! I was expecting the worst all the time—and, well, it's merely postponed."

"The suspense was due to your ignorance of the proceedings," said Costock. "I've sat as a juryman on several occasions, and I've been amazed. Half of 'em appear to have been carved up before they came into court. Perhaps I'm wrong. I dunno . . ."

"I thought Knollis would have been there," said Grayson.

"Not to be expected," said Costock. "Officially he is down here to *assist* the county police. Even in the event of a conviction, which I doubt, he may not give any evidence. The wallah in charge of the county C.I.D., and his uniformed counterpart are the characters who give all the police evidence, apart from such birds as technical experts and pathologists. Y'know—finger-print blokes and the like."

"Finger-prints!" Grayson exclaimed. "If they are working on prints I'm in the clear from the start. Never struck me before. The only prints I could have left were a set from my left hand on the barrel, near the spout, and a right-hand set on the stock. My blessed hands were never at any time near the triggers!"

"I worked that one out from your original story," said Costock. "Mentioned it to Knollis, too. Y'know, just in case genius missed the obvious, as it all too often does. Anyway, we appear to have walked without noticing it, and here is the Falcon—although if that's a falcon on the signboard I've served up a good many of them as Rhode Island Reds at three and six a portion and didn't know the difference."

He opened the swing door for Corinne, followed her in, and held the door for Grayson. "I'm acting as insulator for differing potentials," he murmured softly. Still more softly he murmured: "Look! The gallant colonel himself, straight from Mr. Knollis's quiz programme."

Harry Vere Bolding saw Corinne, and rose to greet her, and, in turn, Costock and Grayson. He ordered drinks and invited them to his table in the lounge bar.

"Had a most interesting morning," he smiled. "The Knollis is a human being under that graven and slit-eyed mask. I honestly think he's on our side so far as opinion of Herbert is concerned—"

He broke off to look round, and then sighed with relief.

"Mrs. Moston not with you, eh? Thought she might have been owing to the inquest, y'know!"

"We're not on speaking terms owing to a slight family difference," said Grayson. He smiled, and added: "You were saying, Colonel?"

"Oh yes, about Knollis! Yes, I'm satisfied that he's in sympathy with our feelings about Moston, but of course the man has his job to do!"

"And consequently you've done what you could to further *his* cause," Costock said caustically.

"Well, I'd hardly put it like that," Vere Bolding protested.

"I would," said Costock. "I know my customers inside out. I also know the admirable Knollis! Do you really think he's gained his reputation as a Master Sleuth by being in sympathy with killers?"

"But dammit—" began Vere Bolding. He glanced at Corinne and said, "Pardon, ma'am!" and continued: "But, dammit, man, I only told him what he wanted to know about the village as I know it as a lifelong resident. It was only the background he wanted."

He paused for a moment before adding: "Crewley's in there now."

"Who fixed that?" asked Costock.

"Crewley," replied Vere Bolding. "You don't blame him for keeping the ball rolling, surely?"

"Reminds me of the Ingoldsby Legends," commented Grayson. "Remember the lines? They go—

The stubborn spearsmen still made good
The dark, impenetrable wood;
Each stepping where his comrade stood
The instant that he fell."

"You have some good friends," said Costock.

"Or Herby had some darned bad enemies," said Grayson. "Who's left for the queue after Crewley—the clot?"

Costock hesitated. "Depends whether you want to feel good, or if you want the truth."

"I'll take the latter. Brother Ignatius would advise it."

"In that case, Longcroft told me that in addition to reading what he told you he read from Knollis's upside-down notebook he read the names of Gwen and Corinne. Beside them was the laconic and hackneyed axiom: *cherchez la femme.*"

"Ridiculous," said Grayson. "Ask Corinne where she was at the time, and that will clear her!"

"Packing," she said across the table. "I told you that once. I think your memory's going—or gone."

Grayson stroked his head. "That's the truest word you've ever spoken! If only I could recall the voice . . ."

Corinne glanced up, quickly. "What voice, Bran?"

"Eh?" he exclaimed. "Didn't I tell you that? Suppose I didn't, considering all things, although everyone else would appear to have the story hand pat. As I started this now famous and disputed walk to Headley Corner, and had just come through the wicket gate, *someone* said good night to me. I answered. I can remember answering, but I can't remember anything else. Haven't a clue as to whether it was man, woman, child or ghost."

Corinne leaned across the table, obviously excited by his calm statement. "Have you—have you told the police?"

"That's a point of interest," answered Grayson. "Have I? I wouldn't know, Corinne. My mind's been like this for a week. I'm sane, but there's something out of gear, and my memory and my reason aren't hitched up. I can remember salient facts as far back as two days ago . . . No, I don't know whether I told the police or not."

"You did," said Costock. "That is why Gwen and Corinne had their names on Knollis's Birthday Honours list. *Vide* Longcroft again, of course!"

Corinne was still not satisfied.

"Bran," she said, "where was this—this person going? Which way?"

Grayson screwed up his eyes in an attempt to remember. He turned to Costock. "Mike, did I tell you it was somebody approaching the gate at the east end of the south wall?"

"That is what you told me," Costock replied.

"Going towards the manor, Bran!"

"If I met them as I was coming away that's a fairly safe inference."

"Then we have only to find who this person was, and we have—"

"A perfectly good red herring to throw to Knollis," Vere Bolding interrupted.

"Pause a while," said Grayson. He pressed the bell, obtained a new round of drinks, and when the waiter had left them he said: "I think we should put the cards on the table. If I ask a question, will all of you, or one of you, answer it truthfully?"

"Of course, old boy," said Vere Bolding. "That goes without saying."

"All right," said Grayson. "Then answer me this; am I correct in saying that all of you, and the whole of the village, believe that I killed Herby Moston?"

Corinne looked away, avoiding her husband's eyes, and her teeth bit deeply into her lower lip.

Vere Bolding herrumphed, and occupied a space of time in rumpling the pile of the red carpet with the toe of his brogue.

Costock grimaced as if the question was distasteful. After a moment he said: "Bran, you ask the darn silliest questions!"

In an ice-cold voice Grayson repeated his question, adding: "I'd like an answer, please."

Costock sighed deeply. "All right, cock! The straight answer is Yes."

"Thanks for that," said Grayson.

"Yes, we know you did," continued Costock, "but in the extenuating circumstances, and considering our own opinions of Herby, we're all determined that *They* aren't going to get you for it."

Looking straight at Corinne, Grayson asked: "Could I ask for a definition of the extenuating circumstances?"

Again there was a long silence, and this time it was broken by Vere Bolding after several embarrassed coughs.

"Point is, old boy, that you weren't quite your usual charming self. Brain-storm and all that. Circumstances pilin' on top of each other and then pilin' on you. The human brain's a tough thing considerin' the delicate nature of its structure, but it'll only stand so much. From the moment you left the Mow you didn't know what you were doing—sorry, old boy, but you did ask for the truth, and I don't think you're the type to dissemble the question."

Grayson looked at Costock. "Well, Mike?"

Costock shrugged. "I guess the Colonel's right, Bran, but they ain't going to get you."

"And Corinne?"

It took Corinne some seconds to speak. Her lips moved as if she was trying to force words from them, and no words emerged. At last she said, reluctantly: "What else can I think, Bran?"

Costock glanced keenly at Grayson. "For God's sake don't look like that at us!"

"I must be a charming friend and husband," said Grayson.

"What are you going to do about it?" Costock asked in a practical tone of voice.

"O beata solitudine! Sola beatitudine!" said Grayson.

"What's that in common or garden English?" asked Costock.

Grayson cocked an eyebrow. "That? I saw it on a tile let into the portico of a house in southern Italy, in Calabria, in the village of Isola Capo Rizzuto to be exact. It's a cry from the heart praising beautiful solitude—and that's the answer. I'll see you at the Barley Mow in about an hour and a quarter from now. I'm off on yet one more of my famous walks wherein I commune with my soul, or the Father within me, or Aladdin's genie, or my secret self, or whatever it is that has apparently accompanied me throughout the ages. It's the only thing I can depend on in this life. It's never let me down once. To outsiders it may have led me into strange behaviour, but that is between it and me."

He swept his glass from the table and emptied it. "I did not kill Herby," he said, "and the person I spoke to in the darkness was no figment of my imagination designed to add verisimilitude and confuse detectives. I don't know whether the voice I heard was of heaven or earth or of a disordered imagination. I don't know whether it was young or aged, tenor or baritone, contralto or soprano, but by the time I get back to Wingford I hope to know the answer."

"How?" asked Vere Bolding.

"There are certain tricks of the mind which I seldom practise," replied Grayson. "Being a materialist, you wouldn't understand if I tried to explain. They verge on the mystical, and I don't like the mystical. With the famous Brother Juniper I opine that even theology should be reduced to an exact science, and with Rudolf Steiner I opine that all come-hither psychical performances should be performed in the normal state of consciousness, without inducing any degree of trance."

He nodded and turned away. "See you later—chums!"

He strode from the Falcon Inn, and down the winding street to the open road. As he walked he dropped all thought from his mind, and let images from the ante-room of memory flood the silver-screen of his mind. They showed him the scene in the Barley Mow before he left for the manor house, the fight with Moston, and every word spoken by Moston and himself was repeated as if being played back from a tape-recorder. He saw himself walk across Peacock, heard the queer metallic click that caused him to change his course. He saw himself treading the red gravel of the Priest's Walk, open the wicket gate at the end of the south wall, and tread the two steps that led to the road. It was then the voice came from the lightning-riven darkness. It came amidst the continual rumble of thunder, and it was a woman's voice, but one he could not recognise *because* of the thunder. It was high-pitched, anxious, and near hysterical, not unlike that of a woman hastening home because of her terror of the storm. Or one of the girls who worked at the manor, perhaps hurrying back after visiting her mother in the village.

He saw himself walking the road to Headley Corner, his way lit by the scarlet net of lightning that spread over all the sky, seemingly to the uttermost ends of the earth.

But he never reached Headley Corner. There was a byway which led to the left half-way between the village and the Corner, and it was here he stood, hands sunk deep in his jacket pockets while he tried to sort out his thoughts and make some sense of the life he was living.

He snapped a thumb and finger to stay the film, and to let thought continue its normal streaming through his brain like water passing through a mill-race. So that was it!

He quickened his pace, realising that the car bearing Corinne and Costock must have taken the longer route in order not to disturb him. Ten minutes later he walked into the Barley Mow, and went straight through to the kitchen where Costock and the two women were taking late lunch.

"I didn't go to Headley Corner," he said simply. "I thought I did."

Corinne covered her eyes with her hands and began to sob quietly.

"And the voice?" Costock asked.

"A woman's voice," said Grayson, "but I couldn't place it owing to the thunder. It was an anxious, hysterical voice, like that of a girl or woman terrified of the storm. There was an urgency in it, and some note of relief at having met a fellow human being on whatever journey she was taking."

He sighed. "That's all I can tell you!"

Corinne lowered her hands. "Did you—did you . . . ?"

Grayson looked her straight in the eyes. "I don't think I killed him, Corinne. I don't think I went back to the manor, but I'm not sure. I couldn't pull back any pictures from the time I stood at the end of the lane. The time error which is puzzling Knollis can only be explained by the amount of time I spent thinking, or dreaming, or what would you, at the corner of the lane."

"All of which would sound horribly lame in court," said Costock. "Might as well start trying to convert the jurymen to Lahsen's theory of time."

Corinne rose from the table and smiled weakly at Doreen. "You must excuse me. These are times when the conventions must go by the board. I must go out."

She turned to Costock. "Can I borrow the car?"

"Help yourself," said Costock. "It's in the yard."

"Could a friend ask where you're going?" asked Doreen.

"To the cottage, and then to Yeagrave," Corinne replied with an enigmatic smile. "Natalie will be all right. She's playing with the little girl next door."

"Which means she's probably up to the ears in the midden," said Costock in an attempt to lighten the atmosphere. "That child next door is a true lover of the soil. She loves the good earth! She eats it, rolls in it like a dog with worms, and presumably sleeps in it. Your infant will probably be in a thoroughly mucky state when she returns, so Doreen should pull out the damper and have lollops of hot water ready."

His nonsense gave Corinne the chance to slip away without further questions being asked of her. Two minutes later the engine of the car purred to life. The car bucked its way over the bouldered surface of the coaching yard to the roadway, and rolled away out of hearing.

"There goes Shirley Holmes," said Costock. "If she detects in the manner of most women you'll probably be in clink tonight. She obviously has some bee under her bonnet."

"That was your engine," said Doreen as she slid the roast in front of Grayson. "Eat, dear. Something tells me we are in for a few hectic hours, and you'll need all the stamina my cooking can provide."

Grayson's agent, Rosing, arrived by car shortly before half-past two, and the two were closeted in the sitting-room for an hour and a half, after which Doreen served them with afternoon tea. Grayson eventually waved Rosing on his way home, and returned to the kitchen.

He sprawled across a chair, and gave a wry smile. "Life's a darned cussed thing," he said to Costock and Doreen. "In one hand I virtually hold a warrant for my arrest for murder, and in the other the promise of a small fortune and a promising career! Rosing's a wonder. He's not only worked Metro for the filming of two of the Grayson books, with options on the next three, but has got my book royalties shoved up to a flat twenty-five per cent, fixed translation rights of all I've written in no less than five languages, and has radio and television offers. What the deuce do you make of it?"

"Ask Lahsen," Costock said facetiously. "You probably lived all this in the reign of Queen Elizabeth the First, complete with film and television rights. Anyway, now you can smell continual lolly coming over the horizon, what do you intend to do about, first, Wingford, and second, Knollis?"

"About Knollis I can do nothing. He has to sort out his own—and my—salvation. For the second I'd like to borrow the car and go into Yeagrave. But Corinne has it! I clean forgot—and I could have let Rosing run me there."

"Bran," said Costock, "I want to commit an impertinence. I want you to let me act as your agent over this possible purchase of Wingford, for various reasons. For one thing you're a weary man, and in no condition for bargaining, apart from which you're a lousy business man at the best—"

"And secondly," asked the amused Grayson.

"If Gwen knows she's selling to you she may hot up the price after the way you snubbed her last night. Let it become known that Michael Costock was visited by Mr. Herman Rosing, who happens to be the unsuccessful Mr. Grayson's agent, and he brought Glad Tidings, with capital initials for Mr. Costock. I'll start the ball rolling by paying round the house tonight without saying why I'm doing it. That will reach Gwen's ears, and she should put two and two together to make five. Then I'll play the fish called Coltness. Will you let me do that?"

"It sounds sense," Grayson said slowly. "Corinne must be warned or she'll go out of her way to crow over Gwen via the villagers."

"Why tell her?" said Costock. "Kid her on that Rosing's offers to you were all very much in the air, and that he really came to see me. No need to make a liar of yourself if your conscience's tender. Just stay mum. After the family quarrel and marital separation you're entitled to do that."

Costock gave an engaging smile. "I never believe in spoiling a good story for a few sentences, so why not let me suggest that

I am turning country gentleman and dilettante writer, and you are taking over the pub?"

"It could be good fun," Grayson agreed.

"Then I'll ring Coltness straight away. Tonight, in the pub, you start asking me stupid questions about the price of this and that. No more! Just enough to start the thing working. Right?"

Costock went to the telephone and chatted for some time with Coltness about the present-day value of Wingford, adding little touches about the obvious need for opening the house to the public every Sunday for half-a-crown a head in order to meet the rates and taxes, and generally playing a more naive part than could have been played by the naturally ingenuous Grayson.

He scratched his black head as he replaced the handset. "Odd, but I think we're going to get it for a song. Gwen would appear to have sensibilities which were foreign to her husband. She's told Coltness that Wingford must go to someone who fits, someone who will love the old place, and care for it."

"She was happy there in her own way," said Grayson. As an afterthought he said: "She still hates my guts."

"I judged that by what Coltness said," remarked Costock. "Let's nip through to the bar and raid the benedictine while we decide who's to be landlord and who's to be lord of the manor."

XII
Role of Honour

THE PART OF Costock's mind devoted to ingenuity came to life with Grayson's acceptance of the play to be produced for the benefit of Coltness, Gwen, and the village in general. A few minutes before opening time he suggested that it would help the story along if Grayson was to unbar the doors and then take his place behind the counter for a time.

"It's pay night hereabouts," said Costock, "and I doubt if you could cope for long without more experience. So off you go, my victualling friend, and look landlordish. I should warn you that you do not have to look surprised as various characters apparently materialise from thin air and walk on your heels as you return from the door. They've been waiting behind trees, buttresses and walls for the past half hour, swearing blind that I open ten to fifteen minutes later every night. Such is the power of the dry throat and the vivid imagination. Go to it, friend!"

It came about as Costock had prophesied, and for the first twenty minutes Grayson was kept busy filling and refilling pints, and then Costock's regulars settled down in the tap-room to play dominoes and darts, gossiping in between times.

Corinne hurried in a few minutes after Grayson got his first chance to breathe. "Where's the cottage key?" she demanded breathlessly.

"In the door—on the inside," said Grayson. "Wingfordians seldom lock up. It is regarded as a sign that they don't trust their neighbours if they do. What's cooking, anyway?"

Corinne nodded, did not reply, and was gone again. The tyres spurted on the flint road and were gone.

Costock had ambled into the bar. "Obviously in something of a hurry," he commented. "She didn't leave a rice pudding in the oven before she came out this morning?"

"We don't eat rice puddings," Grayson said lightly. "We once had an uncle whose hair grew all the way down his back and had to be plaited into a pig-tail after living on rice from birth."

But although he spoke jokingly there was a serious and wondering light in his eyes. He was about to express his thoughts when Longcroft plodded down the flagged passage, his beret well over one ear, and a red tie blazing out from the background of his turquoise blue shirt.

"Evenin' all!" he greeted them. "Usual for me, and I hope you gentlemen will join me—pardon me calling Costock a gentleman, but I try to be polite. Through in the smoke-room, if you please, cock!"

"Any news, cock?" asked Costock, aping Longcroft's assumed mode of speech.

"Crewley's back. Vere Bolding's back. That wipes up the mob, unless you've a turn coming."

Costock smirked. "My reputation being as pure as the dew and above temptation, or whatever it is that Caesar's wife was, my presence has not been requested by the police, Mr. Longcroft, sir!"

"Crewley's back, eh?" murmured Grayson. "What has he to say about the do?"

"Haven't seen him to talk to. Just saw him flashing past the window in his dog-trap, or whatever they call it—doing at least two miles an hour flat out."

"That's Vere Bolding, you clot," said Costock. "Grayson was asking about Crewley."

"Oh, yes, sorry! Got things on my mind. Crewley went by in his souped-up jalopy at about the same rate, but later. Reckon he'll have something to tell us when he comes in."

"If Crewley's back," murmured Costock softly, "it means the meat is getting near the bone. We must have a meeting of the committee of ways and means. Get into the smoke-room, Shorthouse, or Longcroft, or whatever they call you. Bran, open the gate so's I can get through with the tray. Thanks."

They settled in the smoke-room.

Vere Bolding was the next customer to arrive. He nodded all round, accepted a drink from Costock, and seated himself in his usual corner. The conversation was mainly about crops, the abnormally hot and humid weather, the comparative absence of storms—excepting the weekend electric storm when no rain had fallen, and the possible effect upon the turnips, mangolds, and swedes.

At eight o'clock, his usual time, Crewley had not appeared. At five minutes past eight Corinne came and asked if Brother Ignatius could borrow the car, perhaps until morning.

"He can," said Costock, "but is it permissible for my curiosity to be satisfied?"

"It's old Mrs. Walters. I've got some things for her from the cottage, and Brother Ignatius is taking them to her, and sitting with her until she—y'know!"

"She's going," said Vere Bolding.

"She isn't expected to live until morning, Colonel."

"Poor old gel!" said Vere Bolding.

"Is there anything I can send?" asked Costock. "Brandy or anything?"

Corinne shook her head. "The doctor says there's nothing that can be done. She's beyond the pain barrier, and it's just a matter of time."

"I sort of feel guilty," said Grayson. "I haven't called to see her, but what with one thing and another . . .

"She wants nobody but Brother Ignatius, and the doctor wouldn't let anybody else see her, anyway. But he's waiting . . ."

She hurried outside, and the car was revved up and went away in a series of hiccoughs that made Costock flinch.

Corinne did not return, and Grayson decided she had gone to call for Natalie and take her back to the cottage. He wanted to slip away to kiss Natalie good night, but he also wanted to be present when Crewley arrived with whatever news he might have to tell them. He promised to make good his defection later, and stayed on.

It was nine o'clock when Crewley joined them. Costock fetched his drink and then said: "Let's have it!"

Crewley gave a cracked laugh. "Damned odd! I tried, of course, but I was the only person interviewed who had a cast-iron alibi and couldn't prove that I hadn't. I was the only person left here that night who went where he said he was going. Knollis didn't bother me a great deal about my own movements, and seemed to have checked up on me in advance."

He paused, and his tankard went to his lips as if to stop the further pouring out of words.

"This is no time for stalling, Crewley," Costock said severely. "Time is creeping up on us."

"He means me," Grayson said quietly. "Let's have it, brother!"

Crewley lowered the tankard to the table.

"Knollis shook me somewhat."

"It's one of his habits," said Grayson.

"He wanted to fully understand the Philosophy of Good Sitting Down. He wanted to know the ins and outs of being Sound. He wanted to get into the mentality of people like Herby Moston. The good man is a craftsman, no doubt about that even if we don't like his trade, and he cannot—or could not—understand the Philosophy of Living to Make Brass. He tackled me also about the mentality of poets and writers. He had me there, but in my opinion he only wanted somebody or other to qualify estimates he had already made."

He paused for a moment, and then asked: "Who is Lahsen?"

"A metaphysical philosopher," said Grayson. "Why?"

"Knollis asked if I knew anything about him. Was he one of these ammoral johnnies who do not regard life as sacred? I couldn't answer, any more than I could tell him anything about time that takes no account of clocks. Then he wanted to know about life in Wingford B.M. and A.M.—before Moston and after Moston. Had he interfered much in the life of the village and villagers—peasants as distinct from gentry like our worthy Colonel—"

"Come now!" protested Vere Bolding.

Crewley ignored him.

"The man was as full of questions you wouldn't expect the Yard to ask as *Wisden* is full of cricket answers."

"Now I come to think back," said Harry Vere Bolding, "Knollis talked on somewhat similar lines with myself!"

"The rozzer's on to something," said Longcroft. "I can smell it!"

"Never!" said Grayson with an air of mock surprise.

"The odd thing is that he hasn't called for me," said Costock.

"Not likely to do so," said Longcroft. "He knows you're the educated type, and could stall him even while you were stringing him along."

"Thanks," Vere Bolding said dryly.

Longcroft waved a hand. "I didn't mean anything like that, but Costock's different to you. You've got education, but Costock's got education plus."

"And what's the plus?"

"The wideness of horizon that only a literary artist can have. Your education's static. Costock's is dynamic."

"Thanks again!"

"Trouble is," said Longcroft, reluctant to dismount from his hobby horse, "that you had a good education, and you've done nothing with it since you left school."

"I think," said Costock, "that you are getting deeper and deeper into the mire and it isn't doing anybody any good—least of all Grayson. We're agreed, if silently, that he's right up the creek without a paddle, and something has to be done about it."

He turned to Grayson. "By the way, old chap, if you really want to get your hand in you might renew the drinks."

Grayson took the cue. He collected the tankards and glasses and refilled them. On his return he asked Costock to tot up the amount.

Costock obliged, added: "You'll get into it quick enough when on your own."

He turned to Vere Bolding and asked: "Apropos of not much, Colonel, and off the cuff, what's the manor worth today?"

Vere Bolding stared. "I'd dearly like to ask you why you want to know. Could I do so? Damnably ill-mannered, I know, but having had a stake in the old place, y'know . . ."

Costock nodded confidentially. "I wouldn't like anything to leak out just yet, but my agent, Rosing, came down from town this afternoon. Things are in the air. He brought the beginnings of good news. But as I say, I wouldn't want to jeopardise any future happenings by opening my mouth too wide or too early. You do see what I mean?"

Vere Bolding nodded wisely, having thoroughly understood what Costock had not said.

"You know, Costock, you—or Grayson—would be an excellent type to take over. All the luck in the world, old boy! You asked me a price—and there's a thing if you like! Dunno, I'm sure. Times have changed. Twenty-five years ago the house and gardens'd have fetched ten to twelve thousand. A somewhat smaller place in Nottinghamshire recently fetched only just over two thou! Damned bad show, that! Still, the old order changeth! Upkeep so heavy, and taxes so preposterous, owners are nearly giving these old places away because they're losing money on them. Coltness will probably ask five thousand as a maximum, and with a spot of keen bargaining you may get it down to three thousand five hundred. The land's good, and it pays, but the house is a mortmain, a dead hand lying on any owner's shoulder."

Costock stared contemplatively at the ceiling.

"I think it could be arranged," he said slowly.

"You would take up a mortgage?"

"Add 'of course' and you are correct, Colonel!"

Grayson found the conversation boring, and decided he had just about time to catch Natalie before she went to sleep, so he asked Costock if he could manage without him for half an hour.

Costock played up to him. "I'll leave it with you," he said with a careless shrug. "You make your own pace."

As Grayson walked down the passage Longcroft asked Costock if Mr. Grayson was going to take over the boozer, to which Costock replied that it was too early to say anything like that—especially taking into consideration Gordon Knollis, who in certain ways might oppose the transference of the licence.

Natalie was having the time of her life in a tin bath on the cottage hearth, into which hot water had been poured from an old-fashioned side-boiler.

"Look, Daddy!" she greeted him. "Ever seen a bath like this before?"

He grinned at her. Village life, with its absence of London plumbing, was going to be no great hardship for a little girl of eight.

"Good fun, aren't they?" he said, and knelt beside Corinne, and helped, or hindered, the bathing of his daughter.

"I like this house," said Natalie. "Can we stay here for always, Daddy?"

"Dunno that you'd like it, darling. The novelty may wear off after a time."

"Oh, but I wouldn't get sick of it!" she assured him, and let out a yell as he squeezed the sponge down her back.

"There's one thing I'll promise you," said Grayson. "We're never going to live in a stuffy town again!"

Corinne raised her head. "You mean that, Bran?"

"Why, you want to go back?"

"God forbid! There's—there's something about the country—oh, I can't explain!"

"You don't have to do it," said Grayson. "London nearly killed me. Cities always do. When I go back I feel as if I'm being sucked into the maw of a gigantic vacuum cleaner, and for twenty-four hours I'm suffocated and depressed. It takes me all of that time to swing into my work again. Out here, well, I can write at any hour of the day or night. No, Corinne, come wind come weather we stay in the country."

"Then why did we live in a city?"

Grayson shrugged. "I thought you wanted all the conveniences of a town. Women usually do."

"I did," she said slowly. "Yes, I did! But then I'd never lived in the country. I was afraid of it. It was a place in which to picnic for an afternoon, and then return to what we considered to be civilisation."

She stared into the bath for a moment, and then asked: "What is there about Wingford?"

"It was here before Agincourt, according to Vere Bolding. Its roots are sunk deep into the leaf-mould of the centuries—and centuries of leaf-mould. It has character, the life-soul left behind by countless generations of people who have lived here. It is a world, and when foreigners try to enter they are either ignored or absorbed. We are the kind of people who will be absorbed. For some reason which humbles me, we've already been accepted. That is why the ranks closed with us inside when it became evident that Knollis—"

He glanced at Natalie, chasing a pink celluloid duck round the bath with water-dimpled fingers.

"Of that, wife, more another time. Shall we pull out our infant, dry her and powder her, and carry her on the stout shoulders of her Daddy up the wooden stairs to Bedfordshire?"

"She eats and drinks first," Corinne reminded him.

"Peccavi—I have sinned," said Grayson.

So Natalie was dried and talcumed and made ready for bed. She took her supper on Grayson's knee, while for the hundredth time he narrated how Brer Rabbit got the better of Brer Fox in the adventure with the Tar Baby—suitably trimmed with Graysonisms.

"And Brer Rabbit he hollered out 'Bred and born in the briar patch, Brer Fox,' and he lit it out for home, and it was many a long day before Brer Fox cared to show his face among the other creatures."

"And Brer Rabbit he lay low and said nuffin," said Natalie.

"Which," said Corinne with a significant glance at her husband, "is never a bad thing to do, is it, Daddy?"

"You can't beat doing nuffin," he said gently. "The wicked are helpless, and the wise are baffled if you say nuffin. Of a verity the woman speaks truth, for is it not written in the Vedas that in the silence wisdom speaks? And now the Princess must clean her teeth, and retire to her bed-chamber for the night, to dream of Brer Rabbit and Brer Fox, and the love that Mr. Edward Bear has for the Lady Elizabeth."

"And soon there'll be a new companion for the Princess," said Corinne.

Grayson looked up at her, startled, but in the same smooth tone she went on: "Colonel Vere Bolding has promised Natalie a puppy, a black and white terrier puppy, whose ancestors have lived at Wingford for generations and generations—"

"So that he is related to nearly all the puppies and grown-up dogs in East Anglia," added Grayson.

Natalie suddenly remembered. "Ooh, yes! And he's to be called Bonzo, and Colonel Bolding is giving me a kennel for him, and Auntie Bolding is giving him a basket—a lend one to send back when he's grown too big for it and can use Uncle Bolding's kennel."

"How did Mrs. V. B. become an auntie?" asked Grayson.

"We had to do something other than stay in Herby's presence," Corinne replied. "The V.B.s were very good to Nat and me."

Grayson blinked at his wife's unusual use of the name. "Nat?" he queried.

"Well, it's just that I've come round to one of your own ideas. After all the diminutive isn't quite so dignified, and she is still a little girl."

"Yes," said Grayson, because he could think of nothing else to say.

"Aren't you going to say you told me so?"

"Did I ever?" asked Grayson.

Corinne considered the point, and then conceded it. "No-o, I don't think you did."

Grayson hesitated, and then said: "Herby gave you a rotten time, too, didn't he? I'm sorry, but it only just now occurred to me. I'm sorry, Corinne!"

She stared at him thoughtfully, and nodded. "Thanks for that, Bran. I'll hand it to you for being honest even if you've been blind. Yes, Bran, thanks!"

She turned quickly to Natalie. "And now to bed, young lady."

"On Daddy's back!"

So Grayson lifted her to the table, and turned so that she could climb on his back. Ducking low under the low beams, and the still lower lintels, they navigated the winding stairway, and Natalie was dumped on the bed so that she bounced.

When she had been told, again in Graysonisms, how Brer Rabbit used Brer Fox for a riding horse and went for a visit to the house of Miss Meadows, she was thoroughly kissed and snuggled down for the night. The white-painted door was propped open with a chair, and husband and wife went downstairs to the room used by old Mrs. Walters as living-room, dining-room, drawing-room, and almost everything else.

Grayson, stooging aimlessly around for want of knowledge of how to treat the wife from whom he was estranged, came to the over-laden mantelshelf, an inglorious collection of brass ornaments, crest china, and knick-knacks from Brighton, Blackpool and Aberdovy.

"This envelope is in Herby's writing."

"Yes," said Corinne.

"No letter inside it."

"No, Bran."

"You saw the letter?"

"Yes, Bran."

"Sorry," said Grayson. "I'm rude. We shouldn't be so inquisitive, should we—? Against Brother Ignatius's rules for the right-living man."

"We shouldn't, Bran."

The peculiarity of her tone caused him to turn and stare at her. She was standing at the far side of the room, running a forefinger up and down the smooth surface of a leaf of the aspidistra plant.

"Bran . . ."

"Hm?"

"Will you do something for me?"

"Ye-es, I suppose so. If it's in the rules. What d'y'want?"

"Will you go back to the Mow, and wait there until news arrives of old Mrs. Walters?"

"I was thinking of going back anyway. Why the sudden interest in the old dear?"

"Will you do it without asking questions until—until after?"

Grayson walked over to the door. "As nobody never tells me nothing nohow, I'll go now without asking further questions."

"And come back straight away with the news if she dies before midnight?"

Grayson sighed deeply. "I'll even do that for you, but I'd still like to know why!"

She looked round, a sphinx-like expression on her round features. "In the silence wisdom speaks, and he who keeps silence can do good to others without their being aware of it . . ."

Grayson blinked and took half a step back into the room. "That's not the Vedas! That's from Talbot Mundy's book, *Om.* How did you come across that?"

"I'm a bad wife, Bran, but I've tried to keep pace with your intellectualism—and failed."

"God help us!" exclaimed Grayson. "I think it *is* time I went. Smiting me with my own weapons, eh? Well, I'm capable of humility, and I keep praying for understanding."

He walked quickly from the cottage and down the village street to the inn.

The regulars were in position in the smoke-room, like so many chessmen set out each night in their ordered places to await the hand of the player who should move them across the board. Each was in his own seat, and each had a vessel of his favourite brew in front of him. They all greeted him as if it was his first appearance that evening, and Costock asked in a semi-whisper what was happening anywhere.

"Orders from Corinne," said Grayson. "I'm to stay here, and report back immediately we hear that old Mrs. Walters has passed on to the other world—or wherever we go."

Costock registered surprise. "Corinne, eh!"

He whistled softly. "Didn't know the woman had it in her—with apologies for under-rating her intelligence."

Grayson took his arm and dragged him to the passage where they could talk with less risk of being overheard. "Just what the hell's going on around me, Mike?"

Costock patted his shoulder affectionately. "It's just that you're too dim to realise what good friends you have in Wingford."

"You mean Corinne, or old Mrs. Walters?"

"Now that's what I call a very good question," replied Costock. "Have a drink—have several drinks. Then sit back and wait."

He hesitated, and then asked: "By the by, how's the old thought-box? Still as dark as a coal-cellar?"

"Clearing, but still befogged to some extent. Why?"

"Oh, nothing!" said Costock airily. "Just wondered."

"Go on," said Grayson. "Tell me that in the silence wisdom speaks, and I'll commit mayhem on you."

Costock smiled. "Well, doesn't it? You started that, old man. Don't blame me. I'm learning from you, you see."

Grayson said a rude word to him, a short Anglo-Saxon word, and went to the bar and drew himself a pint of bitter which he carried to the smoke-room to join Vere Bolding, Crewley and Longcroft at the dominoes table in a game of Going to the Wood.

Burton, the village constable, looked in shortly after nine o'clock, and after receiving a signal from Costock he went round to the back of the house to find two bottles of beer and a glass on the kitchen table.

Costock joined him via the bar door, and Grayson noticed that when he returned he was digging his teeth into his lip as if worried about something, but having been snubbed once he asked no questions.

A few seconds later Doreen appeared from the kitchen with a light summer coat thrown cloakwise over her slim shoulders. She passed hurriedly through the bar, and left the house.

Grayson lifted an eyebrow, put down a wrong domino, and was reprimanded by Longcroft.

Fifteen minutes later Doreen re-appeared, and beckoned Grayson from the room.

He shunted his dominoes over to Longcroft. "Play these for me."

"What the dickens is happening?" he demanded of Doreen in the passage.

"Knollis and his merry men are turning the cottage inside out. They're searching for something, and they won't say what it is! They've even made Corinne lift Natalie out of bed while they looked under the mattress—"

"I've had enough of this," exclaimed Grayson. "Be damned to patience, and Taoistic passive resistance. I'll take Knollis and Ellis and bang their b—"

Doreen grabbed his arms and pulled him back.

"No, Bran! Corinne says you are to trust her, and stick to orders. You are to wait for news of old Mrs. Walters. She says— and I don't know what she means—she says that nothing can happen until the old lady dies. Corinne herself is quite all right, and seems mistress of whatever situation there is. Natalie didn't awake, and she's tucked in again."

Grayson shook her off, and walked slowly to the doorway. Burton was standing outside, and appeared to be embarrassed by Grayson's appearance.

"What's happening at my temporary home?" Grayson demanded heatedly.

Burton coughed. "All I can tell you, Mr. Grayson, is that if you go across you won't be allowed to see your missus nor speak to her until the C.I.D. blokes have searched the cottage. I know no more than you do. These plain-clothes so-and-sos don't tell us bobbies anything. We're just the sludge-bumping stooges who do the work and get no credit!"

"But they can't work in that way. It's a free country."

Burton wrinkled his nose. "It looks nice in print, sir, does that. They'll have a magistrate's warrant."

He looked at Grayson with the appealing eyes of a thirsty spaniel. "Think I can dodge back to the kitchen, Mr. Grayson? There's a bottle not touched yet!"

Grayson sucked a tooth. "All right, Burton, I'll play with you. I'll go back to my dominoes."

"Don't blame me, sir, will you?"

"Burton," said Grayson, "I don't think you'd arrest a fly—unless it was driving without a tail light. If you can manage another pint I'll send it through."

Burton considered. "A pint's a lot, sir. A half bottle of blue label be all right?"

Grayson went back indoors and saw to it.

"The cottage is being gone through by the Yard men and others," he told his dominoes partner and opponents. "I'm not allowed to see my wife until it is all over."

"These ruddy rozzers . . . !" said Longcroft. He looked closely into Grayson's face. "Don't keep playing wrong 'uns, Mr. Grayson."

The game was played out, and more beer was drunk, and Grayson became more and more fidgety. Knollis came in, and asked to speak to Grayson privately, and Grayson turned awkward, and refused in a determined and aggressive tone.

"I want to search you," said Knollis.

"You can go jump in the river," said Grayson.

"I'm in possession of a warrant . . ."

"So you think you can do anything you like, Mr. Scotland Yard! All right, produce your piece of paper, and go over me with a fine tooth comb. I'm not normally lousy, but it's possible some-thing might have jumped on to me in the past few minutes!"

"The kitchen—or your bedroom?" murmured Knollis.

"Right here!" said Grayson. "I'm the suspect, of no fixed abode. I live in Wingford, in London, on the open road! So it's here or nowhere, and if you don't like the offer you can frog march me to Yeagrave, taking the turnpike road."

A black cassocked figure turned into the room, removed his skull-cap reverently, and announced: "Dear old Mrs. Walters has passed away."

There were murmurs of sympathy round the room, and Knollis became pre-occupied with the news and seemed to forget his errand with Grayson.

Grayson glanced round and sized up the situation. Now that Brother Ignatius was back, Costock's car would be standing outside the door. Knollis moved so that he was at the far side of the room, his back to the fireplace. Vere Bolding was sitting behind the draught wing against the door, and the iron legged table was in front of him.

He moved behind the little priest, grabbed the table and lugged it into the doorway; then sped down the passage and clambered into the car, ill-treating the gear-box as he steered clear of the two police cars standing at the kerb, and shot along the village at a rate that sent the vicarage rooks whirling into the air with alarmed and protesting squawks. He took the wide bend round the churchyard on two wheels, skidded round the next corner, and slammed on the brakes outside the cottage door.

"Corinne!" he shouted urgently as he ran into the sit-ting-room. "The old lady's dead!"

Corinne jumped from the chair in which she was knitting and pressed clasped hands to her breast. "Oh, God! We've got to work fast, Bran!"

"But what—"

"There's no time for argument," said Corinne. She took her handbag from a drawer in the old-fashioned dresser. "Here's two hundred and fifty pounds I've drawn from my own account—I'd hung on to it for a rainy day—and here's your passport, which is in order. Now get moving, and don't stop to argue, please! For Nat's sake if for nothing else!"

"*Listen*, Corinne," said Grayson, "I've got to know what it's all about."

"It's just this," she said flatly. "So far as I can make out old Mrs. Walters was the woman who you spoke to as you left the manor. She went on to the house, and saw—actually *saw*—Herby murdered! But she was the *only* witness who could prove your innocence. And now she's dead . . ."

Grayson leaned himself against the wall.

"And what was Knollis looking for?"

"The letter that came to her in that envelope you found. It was a notice to quit. She went to see Herby, to plead with him to let her stay, and she saw him murdered. It was the shock of it that caused her to fall and hurt herself."

"And how do you know all this?" asked Grayson.

"I went to see her. That was where I went when Natalie walked in her sleep, and that was what she told me, but when the police tried to ask questions she pretended not to understand what they were talking about."

"And who did kill him?"

"She wouldn't say. She was shocked by the manner of his death, and by seeing it happen, but she was so obviously pleased that fate had stepped in to save her cottage that she was prepared to shield the murderer. Anyway, you have to get out now, and waste no time."

She paused, and looked hard at him as a queer twist came to his lips, one she had seen so often before.

"Bran!" she exclaimed. "You aren't going to do *nothing*, are you?"

"I'm going to stay and see what happens," said Grayson. "Y'know, Corinne, you should never refuse an experience. If you funk it, or dodge, or otherwise refuse it you get the same thing in a different form sooner or later."

He looked back through the doorway. "I wouldn't have got very far, but thanks for the work you've put in. Take these back, my girl, before the cops see them in our hands. They might get wrong ideas! The bloodhounds are already outside the gate, with the friends of the fox in hot pursuit. Ah, well, perhaps they let you write novels in quod!"

"There are times." Corinne said slowly, "when I almost admire your guts. The trouble is that you've got more guts than brains."

"As the future squireen of Wingford Manor," said Grayson lightly, "it would come better from your lips if you said *innards* instead of *guts*."

He walked to the door-mat and beckoned. "Come in, Mr. Knollis! My wife and I were expecting you!"

XIII
Deus Ex Machina

GORDON KNOLLIS entered the cottage slowly, as if giving himself time in which to think out a plan of action. Grayson moved over to the fireplace, lit his pipe, and with one elbow propped on the black slate mantelshelf watched with an air of detached interest that he did not feel.

"You may as well come in," said Knollis, looking behind him, and Harry Vere Bolding, Henry Crewley, and Paul Longcroft trooped into the room.

Knollis took off his grey trilby and hung it on the corner of the framed picture of Mr. Gladstone. He turned a chair, and sat astride it, folding his arms across the back and lowering his chin to rest on them. He fixed his gaze on Grayson.

"This is quite a case, isn't it?" he said. "There's a deal I don't know about the happenings on Saturday night. I've taken statements from Mr. Grayson, and the Colonel, and Mr. Crewley, and Mr. Longcroft; it would appear that there's what we might call a communal desire for me to fail to find Mr. Moston's murderer. You may all have excellent reasons for rejoicing at his departure, but I happen to be a policeman, and my job is to find the person who arranged it in such an unorthodox manner. Most untidy!"

He looked round the assembly and gave a dry smile.

"Most of you have tried to incriminate yourselves, if only temporarily. And that interests me. It means that you know who killed Moston—or think you know—and wish to protect him. The way to hell is paved with good intentions, and you've all been chasing up the wrong path to that region."

Vere Bolding moved forward an inch in the crowded room. "Frankly, sir, I don't think you know up which path we have been chasing, whether right or wrong!"

"Oh, yes, I do!" smiled Knollis. "You all thought it was Mr. Grayson. Well, it wasn't!"

Grayson closed his eyes for a few seconds. Unless he was very much mistaken, Knollis was trying to pull a fast one, trying to work a trick. The more he considered it, the more certain he was about it, but he could not imagine what particular trick was being played.

"You see," said Knollis, "I know the exact time at which Mr. Moston was shot. Three of you—the Colonel, Mr. Crewley, and Mr. Longcroft—could not possibly have been there at the time, because all three were seen by various villagers on their way back to the inn. Mr. Costock was more discreet, but I happen to know he entered the inn by the back door as Mr. Longcroft entered via the public entrance."

Grayson nodded to himself. That eliminated four.

"Who have we left?" asked Knollis. "Mrs. Moston, Mrs. Grayson, Mr. Grayson, and young Miss Grayson. They were the only people who could have been on the premises at the time of Moston's death—well, not at the time of his death, but at the time he was shot."

"Don't be so darn silly!" Grayson said shortly.

"You think I'm being silly?" said Knollis, raising an inquiring eyebrow.

"No," Grayson replied very slowly. "I think you are pulling some neat little trick to force, connive, or otherwise wangle a confession from somebody or other. If the truth's known you haven't a clue to the identity of Moston's killer!"

Knollis did not seem at all perturbed by the accusation. Instead, he gave a dry smile, and went on: "Can you prove you went to Headley Corner, Mr. Grayson?"

"You know I can't!"

"Can you prove that you didn't? Can you prove that you went back to the manor house?"

"Nor that," admitted Grayson, "although I fail to see the reason for the question."

"I've said that only four people could have been on the premises. The Mostons found it impossible to persuade any domestics to live in—due, apparently, to amorous tendencies of which Mrs. Moston was not aware. As soon as the day's work was done the ladies returned to their homes in the surrounding villages. So there could have been only four people capable of killing Moston. Mrs. Moston is out of the question, for she had too much to lose by the death of her husband—materially, at least."

Grayson sighed. "Okay, press on with the action to the inevitable climax. I find your logic interesting, to say the least of it."

He raised his chin sharply. "What about the person I passed as I came away?"

Knollis nodded. "Quite a point, isn't it? You know, it's surprising how many times in these cases we have a shadow character brought on the scene. He's always unrecognised, and imperfectly described. He's tall—or perhaps he was short. He may have been fair, or even dark. His suit may have been light grey or navy blue. But he was there, *of course*! Consequently he must have been the culprit. But it's an odd thing that we never trace him, and the person put in the dock is always the only person who saw him."

He broke off as Brother Ignatius insinuated himself into the company, followed by Costock.

"Do come in, Brother," he said. "You may be able to help me to unravel this case with the aid of some of your philosophic theories."

"It is platitudinous to remark that sarcasm is a low form of wit," the little priest said softly. "So far as really helping you is concerned, that may be possible. Throughout this case, time has been the essence of the contract, as the lawyers say in their long-winded documents. Yes, time has been a factor not to be ignored."

"You said," murmured Knollis to Grayson, "that you would be unable to prove that you went back to the manor house—if that should be necessary?"

"I said that."

"So that you would not be able to prove where your wife was at the critical time?"

Grayson took his arm from the shelf, and stepped forward, the stem of his pipe pointing at Knollis as if it was a pistol. "Now, don't come anything like that!"

Knollis merely smiled at him. "But you don't know where she was, do you?"

He turned to Corinne. "Would you care to tell us where you were, Mrs. Grayson?"

Corinne, to Grayson's amazement, shook her head, and remained silent.

"But you were not in your own rooms in the east wing of the house, were you?"

"I was not," she said simply.

Knollis swung himself free of the chair, twisted it round, and pushed the seat under the table with an air of finality.

"I would like you to accompany me to Yeagrave Police Station, Mrs. Grayson," he said crisply. "There are certain questions I would like to put to you, and this is hardly the place."

"What is this?" demanded Grayson, stepping forward until he was nearly standing on Knollis's toes. "Are you trying to suggest that it was my wife who shot Moston?"

"I'm suggesting nothing, Mr. Grayson," Knollis said in the smoothest of tones. "There are certain factors concerned with—er—time that need answering. If your wife admits that she was not in the east wing of the house, then I'd like to know exactly where she was!"

"But what motive could she have had for shooting Moston!"

"Surely you are in a better position to answer that than I am, Mr. Grayson! Moston had first separated you, and then virtually slung your wife and child out of the house, neck and crop. Before that he had done his best for years to poison her mind against you, and I suggest it was in the hour that he gave her notice to quit that she realised the wrong Moston had done *you*, as well as herself and the little girl."

He glanced across the room at Corinne, who was still standing as if paralysed, with her hands clasped over her heart.

"Women do fight for their men, don't they, Mrs. Grayson? Even though you would not care to lose face by admitting it to him directly, you would still fight for him, wouldn't you? You *have* fought for him, haven't you, Mrs. Grayson?" Knollis purred gently. "You drew money from the bank for him, and dusted his passport, didn't you?"

Corinne turned and looked at Grayson, but he was unable to tell what she was thinking. Her face was a mask, impassive and inscrutable.

"You see," said Knollis in what was apparently a friendly tone, "I'm wondering exactly how far you have gone in your husband's interests, which is why I must insist that you accompany me to Yeagrave!"

He took his hat from above Mr. Gladstone's stern features, and moved to the door. "Mr. Costock will be able to arrange for someone—his wife—to look over the little girl's welfare, because you may be with us for some considerable time."

He took a further step towards the door, and said: "Come along, Mrs. Grayson, please."

Grayson whipped quickly round the table, caught him by the shoulder, and spun him back into the room.

"All right, Mr. Knollis! You win! I shot the bastard, and I wish I'd done it fifteen years ago!"

Knollis regarded him gravely as he smoothed the shoulder of his light grey jacket. "But you can't prove you were at the manor house, Mr. Grayson! How could you have shot Mr. Moston?"

"It doesn't matter about time, and clues, and thick-headed methods of detection," Grayson protested urgently. "I didn't go all the way to Headley Corner. I halted at the side turning down to Coombes' Farm, and thought it out. I knew we hadn't finished with Herby, and never would have finished with him while he was alive. He'd bring more and more trouble to us, and we'd had enough. I decided to go back and settle him once for all. He was still in the gun-room, and I shot him."

From behind the half-open door Costock said quietly: "Bran, you're a damn-awful liar!"

Knollis waved a restraining hand. "A moment, Mr. Costock, please! Mr. Grayson, I must do my duty, and give you the formal warning as required by Judges' Rules—"

"You can cut that out," said Grayson impatiently. "I'll tell you anything you want to know."

"Then *do* tell me how you shot Mr. Moston! I'm most interested in that! I really am!"

Grayson glanced at his wife, and in a tone of near desperation he said: "How the deuce do you think I shot him? I put the gun to my shoulder and fired both barrels into him."

Knollis nodded reflectively, and then shook his head slowly. "It won't do, Mr. Grayson! It really won't do. Moston was wounded in the abdomen, and the shot went *upwards* into his liver and the lower lobe of his right lung. You didn't by any chance have a gun with a curved barrel or barrels, did you? No, I appreciate your motive, and to some extent admire you for your courage, but you did not shoot your brother-in-law, Mr. Grayson."

Grayson stared at him, and flopped helplessly, unable to cope with the situation. "Then—then—"

"I still wish your wife to accompany me to Yeagrave Police Station for questioning."

"But—but—" stammered Grayson.

He took a deep breath to steady himself. "Look, do you intend to charge her with killing Moston?"

Knollis looked pained, as if the suggestion hurt him. "Nothing is certain in this world, Mr. Grayson, unless we consider Mr. Longcroft's three inevitables, and this is hardly the time for ribald levity. I can say no more than that I regard your wife's movements on Saturday night as distinctly suspicious."

Grayson swung round appealingly to his wife. "For God's sake say something, Corinne! Say something! This is—it's impossible!"

The sphinx-like smile crept over her face. "You have taught me the art of non-resistance, and neither tonight, nor tomorrow, will I say anything about where I was or what I was doing on Saturday night. Herbert is dead. I'm glad he's dead, because he was rotten all the way through. You know why he turned us out of the house?"

"Nat cheeked him."

Corinne shook her head. "No, Bran," she said. "I couldn't tell you the true reason, because I knew you would have murdered him then. Gwen was going to town for a few days and—well, Herbert said he'd be lonely . . ."

"The—"

Grayson caught himself in time, and clamped his lips tight together.

"That's why he got rid of you—first. That's why he tried to turn me against you, hoping I'd turn to him as my protector, and the protector of Natalie. I saw him then for what he was, and I smacked his face. God, did I smack his face! And then, after raving and shouting about my base ingratitude, he told me to clear out first thing next morning, and take 'the brat' with me."

"I wish you'd told me," said Grayson. "He would have died even less easily than he did. Oh yes! Herby would have had a fantastic and painful end!"

"Did you tell your sister about this?" asked Knollis in a sympathetic voice.

"I told no one but Brother Ignatius. I had to confide in someone, or go mad."

"You told him after you shot Moston, or before?" asked Knollis.

Corinne bit her lips together, and remained silent.

"I think," said Knollis, "I must make up my mind to charge you."

"For what reason?" asked Brother Ignatius.

"I've known for some days that he was shot by a woman. You see, there wasn't a man on the premises—Mr. Grayson, luckily for him, *was* seen by a courting couple as he stood at the corner of the lane to the farm. He stood there, they told me, as if he was in a trance—so long that his presence embarrassed the couple. Once I knew that fact it was purely a matter of elimination."

Brother Ignatius gave a deprecatory cough.

"What is it, Ignatius?" asked Knollis.

"It would seem that once again I have to force myself to intervene, Gordon," said the little priest.

"I'd prefer you to keep out," said Grayson. "I prefer to run my life in my own way, and that includes the lives of my wife and daughter. A mistake has been made, and a way will be found of rectifying it."

"Oh, but I have no intention of intervening in *your* life, Mr. Grayson," said Brother Ignatius.

"Then what—?"

"I am about to intervene in the life of my friend, Gordon. He intends to take a certain way, and I know that nothing but personal disaster lies at the end of it."

Grayson looked up to see a momentary expression of triumph flit across Knollis's face. It was gone in the split-second, leaving him the graven-faced and academic detective known to the general public. He knew then that Knollis had been playing out a well-considered plan, knowing with all certainty that Brother Ignatius held the solution to the riddle of Moston's death.

Brother Ignatius stared regretfully at his toes, peeping through the leathers of his sandals. "Mr. Moston was most certainly shot by a woman," he said, "but it was neither Mrs. Grayson nor his sister. He was shot by our dear friend, old Mrs. Walters . . ."

"Don't be silly!" exclaimed Longcroft. "The old girl wouldn't have swotted a spider."

"You're surely mistaken!" said Harry Vere Bolding.

"Mr. Moston was not a spider," murmured the priest. "Spiders are clean, wholesome creatures that rid the world of much filth."

Grayson looked round the room. Only two people did not appear surprised at the revelation—Knollis and Corinne. He scratched his head. How long could one live with a woman without getting to know anything about her, anything that mattered? He pulled himself back to earth.

"Mr. Moston had given old Mrs. Walters notice to quit," Brother Ignatius was saying. "In the letter he told her the cottage spoiled the view from his window—"

"Yes, and where is that letter?" Knollis interrupted.

Brother Ignatius fished deeply into the pocket of his cassock, and handed the letter over. "She had it with her in hospital," he said apologetically.

A ghost of a smile crossed Corinne's face.

"We turned the cottage inside out for it," Knollis complained.

The priest ignored him. "I was about to say that the letter was his official excuse for turning out the old lady. Verbally he told her that he was fed up with the—er—rotten swine in the village who treated him like dirt. All they could think about was its age, and traditions. So he intended to ruin the village for all time—that is why I came to Wingford last weekend, the old lady having written to me. Starting with this cottage, he was going to tear down everything that belonged to him but the manor house, and that he swore to ruin before he left the village—as he intended doing. He said he would leave the villagers little enough to boast about, and the people rendered homeless could jump in the river for all he cared."

"I told you what the fellow was like, didn't I?" Vere Bolding demanded of Knollis.

"You told me," said Knollis. "Please go on, Brother."

"Old Mrs. Walters was born in the cottage. She had lived here all her life, and it was her life. In sheer desperation she went to the manor to plead with Moston."

"Then it was—" began Grayson.

"Yes, she passed you by the wicket gate."

"And then?" prompted Knollis.

"She found him in the gun-room, having seen the lights as she crossed Peacock. She pleaded with him, and then this good old woman threw aside the pride for which she was noted and went on her knees to him, begging him to leave her the cottage . . ."

Brother Ignatius paused to murmur a prayer beneath his breath.

"Yes? And then?" Knollis asked impatiently.

"Mr. Moston was cleaning the gun. He pushed the stock against her chest, and tried to push her over, backwards. She grasped the stock, and tried to save herself by pulling herself up hand over hand. Mr. Moston cursed her savagely, and jabbed the stock of the gun hard against her breasts. Her fingers came up to the triggers . . ."

"So that *was* it!" said Knollis.

"She was never sure whether she pulled the triggers by accident, or with deliberate intent. She could only remember that she fell over backwards as the gun recoiled, and that Moston collapsed, grasping at his stomach. She was not sure how she got home, but somehow she managed it, and somehow managed to close the door behind her. She fell then, and was unconscious for some time. In between bouts of unconsciousness she realised that she had killed him—for you must remember that she had been a midwife and district nurse and understood such matters. And so inch by inch throughout that painful night she crept to the fireplace, and so arranged herself that it would look as if she had tripped and hurt herself on the fender. She knew Mr. Longcroft would look for her in the morning." The little priest looked at Knollis with a wry smile. "You suspected that the odd shaped bruise on her chest was caused by the stock of the gun, didn't you?"

Knollis nodded.

"And now," said Brother Ignatius, "in order to save the innocent Mrs. Grayson I have had to break the seal of confession. You knew all the time that the Graysons were innocent of this horrible crime!"

"I'm sorry, Ignatius," said Knollis. "Mrs. Grayson also guessed the truth. I happen to know what she was doing on Saturday night. She went—came—to this cottage to ask Mrs. Walters if she could board herself and the little girl. The old lady was not in, so Mrs. Grayson scribbled a note on a page from her shopping pad, and left it on the table. The constable found it next morning. How *much* Mrs. Grayson knew was my main concern. I regret the method I've had to use, but I had to break down one of you." Brother Ignatius fished in the pocket of his cassock once more and brought out several crumpled sheets of writing paper, which he handed to Knollis.

"It is in my writing, but old Mrs. Walters signed it in the presence of the surgeon and myself. I had hoped it would never be necessary to reveal the truth—but there, the many doors in and out of life are not always for us to choose to close or open."

Knollis glanced at the confession, and put it safely in his pocket. Then he extended a friendly hand to Grayson.

"You've had a rough passage, Mr. Grayson. May the future deal more generously with you."

"It will! Oh yes, it will!" said Brother Ignatius. "The circle of recurrent life has been broken, and new lives now become available to him in the upward swirling spiral of time."

"Talking of time," said Costock, "I think we could all do with a drink, so I suggest we meander to my place . . ."

He broke off.

"I forgot Nat. She's in bed."

He turned to Longcroft. "Hop down to the Mow, my Philistinic friend, and grab a bottle of benedictine from the shelf. Tell Doreen to tell the customers to help themselves at my expense, and bring her back with you. We are going to drink to the memory of a very brave old lady . . ."

Epilogue

WINGFORD MANOR came to life again early the next morning. A telephone call from Rosing confirmed the completion of the contract with the Metropolitan Film Company, and a call by Costock to Coltness made Grayson squire-apparent of the Manor of Wingford in the County of Norfolk. Colonel Harry Vere

Bolding was told the news, also by telephone, and twenty minutes later appeared in the village with his lady wife, who carried with her the terrier pup for Natalie.

Corinne and Doreen took Natalie and the puppy to see their new home, and Grayson, still uncertain of Corinne's attitude to himself, followed after an interval.

There he found Brother Ignatius, standing in the doorway of the Great Hall as if expecting him. Together they went through to the gun-room, and wandered to the open french window.

"So you are free again," said Brother Ignatius.

"Free again," Grayson said contentedly.

"And you are buying the place."

"Yes," said Grayson. "Nat will forget Herby in the course of time. I had that to think about, but as I saw it I had no choice but to bring her here. If she went away from Wingford she would always associate such lovely places with unhappiness. She's highly impressionable, and at a suggestible age, so we'll surround her with beauty, and it's the fragrance she'll remember, and not the thorns."

"That is wise," said Brother Ignatius.

"I'm taking a risk, and the bull by the horns," Grayson went on reflectively. "I'm buying Wingford, and I haven't asked my wife's opinion, and shall not do so. The place is obviously too big for us as it is—and far too expensive—and so we'll keep the east wing intact, and live there. We'll convert the rest of the house into flats without damaging anything that has stood since long before Agincourt. And we'll choose our tenants very carefully!"

Brother Ignatius stared across the grounds to where Corinne and Doreen were walking arm in arm along the Priest's Walk towards Lady Charlotte's Herb Garden.

"And your wife?" he asked softly.

"Brother," said Grayson, "you can't cut down an established tree and expect the wounded stump to sprout new green shoots overnight. The tree will grow again, but it won't be the same tree. Life is persistent. You can neither contain nor suppress it. I'm prepared to wait. It may be a long time, for the older tree has to give strength to the new sapling—Natalie."

He folded his arms, and straightened his shoulders as he stared across his estate.

"Remember what Harry Vere Bolding said about trees? You have to let them grow Nature's way, slowly and steadily, to produce well-hearted wood. If you try to force their growth you produce hollow mockeries of Nature."

"You are indeed truly acquiring wisdom," said the little priest.

"I've prayed for it—that and understanding," said Grayson quietly. "My wife wasn't felled. She was eaten into by acid, the acid of hate poured into her by my enemy. But the poison will be neutralised in the course of time, and the pure clean sap will flow again. As I say, I can wait."

Out on Peacock, child and dog were whirling round each other in a frenzy of excitement, the child laughing merrily, the dog barking and yelping, unconscious manifestations of the all-pervading, ever-present spirit of life which was, and is, and will be, even unto the end of the world.

THE END